The Da

By Ian Wright

The Dark Reckoning

First Edition, October 2013

Copyright © 2013, Ian Wright

All Rights Reserved. This book may not be reproduced in any form, in whole or in part, without written permission from the author.

Use of the Sherlock Holmes characters created by Sir Arthur Conan Doyle by permission of Conan Doyle Estate Ltd., www.conandoyleestate.co.uk.

All characters and events in this book are fictitious. Any resemblance to persons, living or dead, events, places or organisations is unintentional and entirely coincidental.

Printed by CreateSpace, An Amazon.com Company

This book is dedicated to everyone who offered support and encouragement whilst I was writing it, especially my sister, Jacqui. I thank you all.

The Dark Reckoning

Chapter 1

The cold December air chilled the fingertips of Sherlock Holmes, as he hurriedly walked along the cobbled streets of London towards Baker Street. As he approached Marble Arch, he noticed that a crowd had gathered just inside Hyde Park. Curiosity, as well as a distinct lack of investigations, led him to walk across Park Lane to determine the reason for such a presence.

Sherlock Holmes was one of the most renowned private detectives in London, and was often called upon to help solves crimes that baffled the police. He was a restless man, 40 years of age, who could not abide idleness. For

Chapter 1

several weeks there had been no cases that were of sufficient interest to him, causing him to become increasingly depressed and frustrated. His apartment showed signs of his frustrations, being littered with newspapers and records of old cases all over the floor. His landlady had been kept busy trying to tidy up after him, a habit that he found infuriating as nothing was ever where he left it.

Waiting for an approaching carriage to pass, Holmes noticed the panting of its two horses as they cantered by, the heat of their breath causing steam to issue from their nostrils. The driver of the carriage was wrapped in a thick cloak and was wearing his hat low, so that only his eyes and grimy cheeks showed between the garments. He appeared very weather-beaten and Holmes guessed he had worked outside for many years. He seemed impervious to the bitter coldness in the late afternoon air.

Holmes crossed the road, noticing that the street lamps were being ignited. He entered Hyde Park by Cumberland Gate and made his way towards the crowd. Weaving his way through the dense mass of people was no easy task, even for the slim built Holmes. Owing to his height, just short of six feet, he did not have to advance too far into the crowd before he could see over the heads of the onlookers. Several feet in front of where he stood, a wall of policemen shrouded a figure lying perfectly still on the ground. With a strange mixture of frustration and excitement, Holmes pushed himself forwards through the people and made his way towards one of the policemen.

The Dark Reckoning

"I'm sorry Sir, but I can't let you pass. Please move along now," said the policeman in an authoritative voice.

"Who is in charge here?" snapped Holmes somewhat impatiently, having become somewhat agitated after fighting his way through the crowd.

"Inspector Lestrade," replied the officer.

"Well, where is he, man?" asked Holmes in a raised voice

"Over there, Sir," said the officer pointing the inspector out.

"Thank you. Now, will you *please* let me pass?" said Holmes, pushing his way past the policeman, who immediately tried to restrain him and pull him back. "Lestrade!" shouted Holmes.

Inspector Lestrade glanced over and saw the welcome figure of Sherlock Holmes. "Ah, Holmes, I'm glad you're here. It's alright officer, you can let this man pass". Holmes noticed the strain evident in Inspector Lestrade's face. He was a shorter man than Holmes and stood 5 feet 7 inches. Holmes did not know his age, but thought him to be in his mid forties. He had dark brown hair that was hidden under a hat. His hair was beginning to turn grey at the temples, as were his rather long sideburns. Although not fat, he did have a potbelly and his nose was always red, indicating that he was a frequent drinker. He had lived in London all his life and was from a working class family, which was evident in his accent.

Chapter 1

Lestrade began to speak as the two men walked towards the figure being shielded by the wall of police. "It's a nasty one, this. I hope you haven't just eaten anything".

Holmes quickly smiled his acknowledgement and then looked down at the figure lying on the grass. It was that of a rather stout man wearing very expensive clothing; shoes made of the finest leather, and, beside the body, a cane embossed with a silver handle fashioned in the shape of an Alsatian dog. A cloak made from tweed, and a marriage ring on a chubby purple finger suggested this had been a wealthy man. All this Holmes noticed in an instant, as his eyes were drawn towards the body's head; but it was not there.

After a few seconds of sickening shock, Holmes composed himself. Regaining his great reasoning powers he wondered why, on such a cold day, this man should be out without gloves on. "Was this crime committed here?" he asked, looking back at Lestrade.

"No, there is evidence to suggest the victim was dragged here," replied Lestrade, pointing to marks present on the grass. Holmes saw that it was futile to follow the trail since the crowd had trodden it in too much.

"Damn!" he whispered to himself. He stared into the assembled crowd angrily and then looked back at the body. "May I please examine the body, Lestrade?"

"Erm, I suppose so. Just don't touch anything. You know what the chief can be like," replied Lestrade, somewhat hesitantly.

The Dark Reckoning

Holmes nodded in agreement and knelt down to take a closer look at the decapitation wound. The cut appeared fairly clean and there were two lines visible across the wound, one about half way through the neck and the other just cutting into the spine. This suggested that an instrument such as a meat cleaver had been used to cut off the victim's head. The angles of the lines were slightly diagonal with the right-hand side, as one looked from the end of the body, being inclined towards the ground. Furthermore, the bottom of the initial cut was about one quarter of an inch further into the neck than the top of the second. Holmes deduced that the murderer must have been right-handed and, owing to the depth attained with each cut, suspected it to be a particularly strong male. The spine itself had been struck several times with the blade but it didn't appear to have been cut completely through. It appeared as if, after several attempts to cut through it, the murderer had twisted the head violently to snap the spine.

The light was beginning to fade too much for Holmes to continue investigating and nightfall was gradually drawing in. He stood up and, as he did so, noticed that the cloak of the dead man was not damaged, except for a small amount of blood immediately in the area of the wound. Also there was not much blood on the ground, confirming Lestrade's earlier statement that the murder had been carried out elsewhere. Perhaps the victim had been abducted and held prisoner for some time, thus his cloak was not on his person when he met his end. "Are there any clues as to his identity, Lestrade?" enquired Holmes.

Chapter 1

"We think it might be Sir Charles Grey, the Tory politician. He was reported missing a few days ago. Without a head, though, we can't really be sure that it is him."

"Yes, I read of his disappearance in the newspapers. Where is the body to be taken?"

"It will be taken to the city morgue. Why do you ask?"

"Oh do come along, Lestrade! You surely don't imagine that I will decline the opportunity to conduct my own investigation into his murder? I will leave you now, but please be assured I shall be contacting you."

Holmes smiled, as he turned and walked away in the direction of the trail where the body had been dragged. It proved to be a fruitless venture as the trail had been obliterated by the crowd, many of whom appeared quite desperate to see what had happened. Holmes continued in the same direction, but could not pick up the trail and, after a short while, he gave up his efforts.

Continuing his journey home, Holmes walked briskly along Oxford Street. He looked around him at the horse-drawn carriages scuttling around the streets and all the people walking in different directions, each with their own purpose. He wondered if anyone knew anything, but concluded most were too wrapped up in their own affairs to have noticed much. He saw a tramp begging for money from anyone who passed close by him. Holmes observed that most people simply gave the tramp a disapproving frown and offered him nothing. Holmes thought it possible that the tramp had seen something of what

The Dark Reckoning

happened in the park. He ventured towards the tramp and offered him a few coins. The tramp immediately gave a toothless smile to Holmes.

"Thank ya, Sir! It...it's so cold. This'll pay for me bed tonight. I didn't much fancy gettin' meself stuck out 'ere," said the tramp, with appreciation.

"I quite understand," acknowledged Holmes. "Tell me, did you see anything of that awful business inside Hyde Park?"

The tramp suspiciously eyed Holmes and then looked quickly from left to right. "Are you the police?" he asked awkwardly.

"No. My name is Sherlock Holmes and I am a private detective. It would help me if you could tell me anything that you know."

"Yes Sir. I did see somfin," added the tramp.

"Go on," prompted Holmes.

"It was 'orrible. I saw it. The bloke didn't 'ave an 'ead. And I'll tell ya somfin else. There was..." The tramp suddenly stopped talking.

"Please continue," prompted Holmes.

"No! I said too much already."

Holmes thought for a moment and then removed a pound note from his wallet. He held it out to the tramp, who

Chapter 1

made a sudden grab for it. Holmes quickly withdrew his hand and looked the tramp in the eye.

The tramp studied the face staring at him. It was rather long and thin in appearance, with a slightly prominent nose. It was a very distinguished face and gave the impression that its owner was a man of great intelligence. The eyes were dark and piercing. They were staring at him in the most uncompromising manner and it made him feel uncomfortable. The thin lips slowly broke into a smile and the detective started to speak. "Tell me what you know and I shall give you this pound note."

"What? Really? You ain't jus' kiddin' me?" asked the tramp, his eyes wide with anticipation.

"Of course I'm not. Now please, I *implore* you. Tell me what you know," replied Holmes.

The tramp again looked left and right, as he considered the offer being presented to him. It didn't take long. "Well Guv, it's like this. I saw this coach go past. Posh one it was. Anyway, I watched it go up the road an' in the park gates. I 'ad a walk up, like, to see if it 'ad stopped."

The tramp paused and spat onto the pavement. "It 'ad stopped, so I went up to it to see if I could beg a few pennies, like. Anyway, I catched up wiv' it and saw someone was in it. The bloke inside said I could 'ave ten shillings if I 'elped the driver move this sack that was inside. Bloody 'eavy it was too. So we moves it out of the coach and onto the grass. The bloke pays me an' tells me to clear off."

The Dark Reckoning

"What happened next?" asked Holmes.

"Well, I walked off like the bloke said, but I didn't clear right off, no Sir! I hid behind this tree and watched 'em. There was two of 'em and they made out they was working on a bush, like they was trimmin' it. They was doin' that for a long time until no-one was about." The tramp stopped talking and looked down at his feet.

"So, what did they do when they believed there was nobody else about?" asked Holmes, now genuinely intrigued by the tramp's story.

"They dragged the sack about 20 yards, maybe. Then they opened it wiv a knife and tipped it over, and..." The tramp paused, looked at Holmes and then continued, "So, they tipped it over and a body fell out! It was a *dead* bloke!"

Holmes remained silent for a moment, before asking, "Did you see what these two men looked like?"

"No Sir, it's me eyes. They ain't what they was."

"Were they well spoken?"

"One of 'em was; the one that gave me the ten shillings, but the driver never spoke."

"Can you describe anything about them to me?"

"Not much. Me eyes really ain't good. The driver was big, really big and very strong. The other one 'ad 'is coat done up tight and 'is hat pulled down low, so I didn't get

Chapter 1

much of a look at 'im. He stayed in the carriage while I 'elped the driver move the sack."

"I see," said Holmes thoughtfully. "What time did all this happen?"

"I can't tell the time, Guv. It weren't long ago. In between when the clock struck three times and four times."

"Thank you for your help," said Holmes thoughtfully. "Here is your pound note. Oh, by the way, you don't still happen to have the ten shillings, do you?"

"No, Guv."

"Never mind. Once again, thank you for your help. Goodbye."

"Cheers, Guv."

Holmes left the tramp and continued his journey to Baker Street, where he rented an apartment. He was glad to leave the tramp, whose smell had been overwhelming.

It was almost dark as Holmes drew close to Baker Street, the skyline of buildings and treetops were silhouetted against a dark blue sky. There were thousands of stars visible, like bright glittering speckles in a vast expanse of indigo. A few wispy clouds looked like ghosts haunting the moon, being gently illuminated by its glow.

The bright warm glow of gas street lamps was diffused by the frostiness in the night air. In the street there was a

The Dark Reckoning

fresh pile of horse manure, sending ribbons of steam up into the cold atmosphere. A man walked across the street, gazing into the irresistible light of an upstairs window; hoping to catch a glimpse of clandestine activities within. With his gaze firmly fixed on the window, the heel of his foot landed heavily in the manure. The man's foot slid a little, causing him to stumble, and he quickly looked around hoping that nobody had seen him.

Holmes saw what happened and tried to suppress his mirth, as he didn't want the unfortunate chap to see him laughing. He walked passed the man, who was trying to look as dignified as possible, as if nothing had happened. Holmes had to bite his lip to stop himself from bursting out laughing as he walked by. The man wiped his shoe on the curb and then began to follow Holmes, until turning off into a side street.

It was from a side street that Holmes heard a sarcastic, mocking voice say, "The game's a head, Mr. Holmes!"

Holmes turned suddenly, staring into the darkness from whence the voice came. He ventured into the side street and saw a figure run into the labyrinth of streets and alleys, rendering pursuit difficult. Holmes gave chase, but the figure had a substantial head start. Holmes, being a tall man with a long stride, began to catch up with the figure, who kept turning into different side streets and alleys. Holmes felt his heart pounding but saw his prey getting closer, although he was still quite a long way ahead. Every time he turned a corner, Holmes lost sight of him for a short while.

Chapter 1

The figure turned into an alley and Holmes followed. The alley split into two and, as Holmes reached the split, he stopped to see which way the figure had gone. There was a figure running from him in both directions. Instant confusion caused Holmes to pause, not knowing which person to pursue, until both had disappeared into the night.

"Damn it!" growled Holmes under his breath. He made his way back to Baker Street, as he recalled the words 'The game's a head'. The voice was gruff, that of a male. It had been spoken with a slight cockney accent, which had seemed laboured, as though false. Perhaps this man knew something of the decapitated body. If so, why should he associate Holmes with it?

Holmes arrived at 221b Baker Street looking somewhat perplexed. He stood on the doorstep fumbling around in his pockets for his keys, which he eventually discovered and promptly dropped onto the step, as his fingers had become so cold. The door was opened from within by a small, tubby woman, about sixty years of age. Her silver grey hair caught the light shining from the porch. Her round face looked puzzled as she stared at the man stooped down in front of her. She spoke with a faint Scottish accent, "Aye, I thought I heard you fumbling. Whatever are you doing, Mr. Holmes?"

"I'm looking for my keys, Mrs. Hudson. Ah! Here they are. Good evening Mrs. Hudson," said Holmes standing up and smiling. He looked at the kind face of Mrs. Hudson, which seemed somewhat worried. She waved her arm to beckon him in. "Well come in out of the cold, Mr. Holmes. Are you hungry?"

The Dark Reckoning

"I am starving, Mrs. Hudson!" exclaimed Holmes. "I have been looking forward to sampling some of your delicious cooking."

The worried look on Mrs. Hudson's face dissolved into a smile, as she listened to the rather unexpected compliment about her cooking. "Whatever are we going to do with you, eh? I'll cook you something up, Mr. Holmes, and bring it to you shortly."

Holmes stepped through the doorway into the entrance hall. He flashed a smile at his landlady and responded, "Thank you, Mrs. Hudson. I don't know how I would ever manage without you."

The great detective quickly ascended the stairs, barely noticing the décor of the hall, which consisted of a very expensive carpet plus two Indian rugs placed along its length. The walls were covered in a deep red paper patterned tastefully with gold leaf. Several paintings lined the walls, as well as an ornately framed mirror close to the main door. There were two oak cabinets, upon one of which stood a clock, its pendulum swinging in perpetual motion. The glass doors of the cabinets displayed several ornaments, collected from around the world. Just inside the front door stood a hat and cloak stand that Holmes never made use of.

Holmes reached his apartment door and went to open it, but instead paused. He smiled to himself and knocked sharply on the door and waited for it to be opened.

Dr. John H. Watson sat dosing in an armchair. He had a fairly stout build with a round face and stood 5'9" tall.

Chapter 1

He was 38 years of age and had a thick brown moustache, which matched the colour of his hair. His hair was wavy and parted on the left side. Bushy eyebrows framed his blue eyes.

A loud knock on the door awoke him with a start. He stretched, stood up and lazily moved towards the door and opened it.

"Ah! Watson, you will never guess how eventful my journey home was!"

Watson observed the figure filling the doorframe. A tall man with a deerstalker in his hand and shiny jet-black hair, oiled and combed straight back over his head. The man had a glint of excitement in his eyes as he stared directly at Watson.

Watson yawned and stretched his arms. "What happened, Holmes?"

Holmes began to recount all that he had seen on his way home. He told Watson of the headless corpse, the man who had said 'The game's a head, Mr. Holmes' and of the man who stepped in the horse manure.

When Watson had finished laughing about the man who 'bore the aroma of a soiled stable', as Holmes had described it, he prompted Holmes to continue, by asking, "What do you make of it all, old fellow?"

"Well," Holmes paused, relishing the curiosity evident in Watson's gaze. "My initial observations and deductions are as follows. Firstly, the man who spoke the words 'the game's a head, Mr. Holmes' appears to have been waiting for me to pass. He probably knew when I would happen past the side road in which he concealed himself. Furthermore, this man recognised me. Since his voice and accent both sounded disguised, it is possible that I may know this man, and he was attempting to conceal his identity from me. The words he spoke suggest that he knew about the murder in Hyde Park and, also, that I would be there!" There was a sudden increase in the tone of Holmes' voice as his mind made a connection between what had seemed to be two entirely unrelated events. "I'm being carefully led into a trap, Watson!" he blasted with a curiously joyous excitement.

Watson's shock and confusion were immediately apparent on his face as he questioned, "Well, go on Holmes. How did you arrive at *that* conclusion?"

Holmes crossed the room to the table where he had cast his cloak upon his entrance, burying a pile of books, drugs and hypodermic syringes that had been left scattered there. He picked up the cloak and reached into a pocket and pulled his hand back out. His eyes shone with excitement as he showed what he was holding to Watson.

"This, Watson! This is how I arrived at my conclusion!"

"A piece of paper?" queried Watson, sitting back down in his chair. "I don't understand."

There was a knock on the door, followed by the familiar voice of Mrs. Hudson as she said, "Your supper's ready, Mr. Holmes."

Chapter 1

Holmes went to the door, dropping the piece of paper in Watson's lap. "Read it," he said as he opened the door. "Thank you Mrs. Hudson. Ah! Shepherd's pie. Splendid! Please do not disturb us again this evening, Mrs. Hudson."

"But, what about your plate, Mr..."

"Thank you, Mrs. Hudson!" interjected Holmes, shutting the door. He turned to Watson, his thin lips breaking into a smile. "Well, what do you make of it, old man?" he asked, as he sat at the table and began to eat.

"Erm, well I don't know. It just reads, '*Be at Prince of Wales Gate, Hyde Park at 4:00pm on Wednesday 7th December 1881*'. Today's date. So what?"

"Don't you see, Man?! Look at the handwriting. Notice how each letter has been carefully written in a different style. Also, notice the smudging of the ink from left to right. This, together with the lack of uniformity in the pressure used by the author to hold the pen, leads me to one obvious conclusion. The person who wrote it used their left hand, but is, by nature, right-handed. Furthermore, but of course you do not know this, I arrived at the Prince of Wales Gate at 3:55pm this afternoon and waited until a quarter past four. During that time, nobody approached me. It may be a coincidence, but I think that the person who wrote this note, in handwriting clearly disguised, knew that a murder would take place. By inviting me to a false appointment, the writer manipulated me into discovering the body. I believe that my adversary is known to me; hence the disguised handwriting. If the man in the side street, who said 'the game's a head', is also the author of this note, then I am doubly sure that he knows me. I wonder whether the person, or people, expected me to deduce this much, or perceive me as somewhat more asinine," ventured Holmes, thoughtfully.

"Why do you suppose the author of the note included the year? That seems a little fastidious to me" asked Watson.

"I thought the same, my friend. It looks as though we are dealing with a particularly meticulous character. Or, at least, that is the impression being conveyed."

"Well, that is quite a comprehensive scenario, old chap," commented Watson.

"Yes, isn't it?" asked Holmes, rhetorically, as his mind considered the events, trying to make more sense of everything.

Chapter 2

Chapter 2

The room was laden with books; books on criminology, criminal psychology and reference books on a wide variety of subjects. There were scientific books, and approximately two hundred files containing newspaper articles with details of crimes committed throughout many years. Yet more files contained notes and documents relating to criminal cases.

A small table in the corner of the room was littered with beakers and conical flasks, all evidence of time consuming experiments that had been carried out. A tall cabinet, with glass doors, contained sealed bottles of chemicals, all of which should have appeared out of place within a living room. Contrary to that, these items added

The Dark Reckoning

a certain character to the room that, somehow, suited its occupier.

The furniture, although not extravagant, was tasteful and of high quality, comprising of two high backed armchairs and a three seater sofa. There was a dining table with four chairs. Upon the table was a dirty plate with a knife and fork. Most of the table was buried under a large pile of books and, in one corner, there was a small box containing drugs and hypodermic needles.

A dark grey cloak was draped across the back of one of the dining chairs, left where its owner had thrown it upon his arrival the previous evening.

The fireplace had an ornamental mantel, upon which stood an old pendulum clock, surrounded by a number of artefacts collected from around the World. The coal fire was being stoked up by Mrs. Hudson, whilst Holmes, wearing a red smoking jacket and supporting a pipe between his lips, drew the curtains back. The morning sunlight flooded in through the east facing window bringing a cheerful brightness to the room. Having successfully started the fire, Mrs. Hudson smiled at Holmes and left the room, taking the dirty plate with her.

The apartment consisted of this room, two bedrooms and a bathroom; the kitchen being downstairs in the main house, which was occupied by Mrs. Hudson.

"Good morning, Holmes. Did you have a good night's sleep?" enquired Watson, as he entered the room.

Chapter 2

"Yes, thank you, old fellow. Mrs. Hudson should return presently with the breakfast and the morning papers. I wish to ascertain all I can of the murder victim from yesterday before we go."

"Go? Go where?"

"We are going to the morgue, Watson. I wish to take a closer look at the corpse. The light was beginning to fade when I looked yesterday, so I may have missed certain details."

Watson broke wind just as the door opened and Mrs. Hudson entered, carrying a large tray with the breakfast. She gave Watson a disapproving stare, but chose not to say anything.

"Really, Watson!" exclaimed Holmes, "I do apologise about Watson, Mrs. Hudson. Do you have the morning papers?"

"I'll bring them shortly, along with a pot of tea, Mr. Holmes" replied Mrs. Hudson, as she and the detective exchanged a smile, caused by Watson's increasing embarrassment.

"Shall I open a window, Mr. Holmes?" asked Mrs. Hudson, still smiling. Holmes shook his head so she left, returning a few moments later with the tea and papers. Holmes read through the papers as he ate. He did not discover a great deal, except that the head had not been found.

The Dark Reckoning

"Come along, Watson!" insisted Holmes, having barely finished his breakfast.

"But Holmes, I haven't finished my breakfast!"

"Well, hurry up then!"

Watson mumbled under his breath as he forced the last mouthful of toast down.

Out in the street, the sun shone brightly and the air was crisp and cold. Patches of frost glistened in the morning sunshine, not yet melted by its weak heat. Holmes and Watson joined the crowds of people walking along Baker Street. Several of the men, including Holmes, were attired in double-breasted coats, top hats and gloves. Watson preferred a tweed coat and bowler hat. The women mainly wore cloaks over their colourful dresses. Most wore bonnets and gloves, some of which were too thin to offer much protection against the cold. Some also carried small umbrellas to shield themselves from the bright sunlight.

It was an invigorating morning, so Holmes and Watson travelled at a lively pace to keep warm. The streets were full of horse-drawn carriages, conveying passengers to their destinations. The buildings rising high above the street were of various architectural styles, ranging from the very old to more recent.

The two men continued along Baker Street and into Orchard Street. When they reached the end, they turned left into Oxford Street and then right into Regent Street. After a short walk along Regent Street, they turned into

Chapter 2

the maze of tiny side streets. As they navigated their way through the back streets, Holmes noticed the transition in the area. Here, the buildings were old slums, decaying remnants of an age gone by. The two men walked through narrow passageways where the buildings loomed overhead, creating an oppressive atmosphere. The buildings prevented much sunlight reaching the passages, which made it feel much colder, and more depressing. This was where many of the poorer inhabitants of the city lived, discreetly hidden from view, so as to make it easier for the wealthy to forget about.

The contrast between this and the busy, bustling streets they had just left was alarming. Although most people avoided these streets, and spent little time even acknowledging them, such areas existed all over London, serving as a sad indictment of a ruling class that didn't care. The buildings sagged under their own weight, once proud roofs now drooped between their supports. Missing slates allowed rain to enter and rot the timbers inside. Broken drainpipes hung precariously above. Many windows were either boarded up or cracked, and most were too grimy to see through, thus providing an effective barrier to keep the poverty within out of sight.

Holmes knew this type of area well, as it attracted so much crime. Theft, extortion, prostitution and murder were all commonplace. So many crimes went unnoticed, simply because the authorities decided that the victims didn't matter enough to bother about. Useless wretches choked on their own vomit as they lay oblivious to the World in opium dens; pathetic carcasses believing they had nothing to live for.

The Dark Reckoning

Some of the alleys in this area were only a few feet wide, with buildings looming up on either side. Holmes thought that these buildings somehow mimicked the ruling classes with their ability to suppress those unfortunate enough to dwell within.

Ahead of the two men, a small group of children were playing in an alley by skidding across a patch of ice. Their clothes were little more than dirty rags, but their faces were smiling, until they noticed the two well-dressed gentlemen approaching. The children stopped playing and eyed the two men with suspicion. Holmes approached them and offered each a farthing. He knew that if he gave them any more, it would probably be stolen from them and they may get hurt in the process. They all smiled up at him with appreciation, though their happy dirty faces could not conceal the sad, sunken eyes and gaunt, pale features.

"Why did we have to come this way, Holmes?" asked Watson with compassion, although he already knew the answer.

"Is it not obvious, Watson?" Holmes replied, sadly, "These people should not have to live like this. The abject poverty in this area is overwhelming, and I find it utterly abhorrent. How many of those children that we just passed by will die before reaching adulthood? I can already see the effects of living in such disease-ridden squalor in their young, tainted eyes. How many of those children will end up lying dead in the arms of their weeping mothers? What crime did these children commit to deserve such a miserable existence? They committed no crime."

Chapter 2

Holmes became silent as he surveyed the area. The two men had stopped walking as Holmes looked around, slowly shaking his head.

He turned to Watson and continued, "I feel as though all the people who end up here indirectly pay, in suffering, the price required to keep the privileged few on their luxurious pedestals. There is so much crime here, but it's mostly committed out of *shear* desperation; mothers turning to prostitution and fathers stealing whatever they can just to provide their children with a few scraps of food. It's all so ugly, Watson, and I cannot abide the society that allows it to continue."

The two men continued their journey through the grimy alleys and under derelict arches in silence. The dark brown brickwork, covered in grime, seemed to reflect the dark mood Holmes found himself in.

Eventually, they arrived in Haymarket, the pleasant environment a complete contrast to the squalor they had left behind. They turned into Pall Mall, and continued on to Trafalgar Square, and then, Whitehall. They passed by Scotland Yard and, a short distance later, arrived at the morgue.

Inside, they were greeted by a very tall, thin man with grey hair. His skin was wrinkled and there was a slight grey pallor to his complexion. His cheeks were sunken, giving the impression that his skin had been stretched over his cheek bones. His dark brown eyes were set back in his head and looked dull. He was wearing a blood stained overall that had, originally, been white.

The Dark Reckoning

Upon seeing Holmes and Watson enter, he smiled and said, "Good morning, Gentlemen."

"Good morning, Dr. Death," replied Holmes.

"What can I do for you, Mr. Holmes?"

"Have you received the body found in Hyde Park yesterday afternoon, Doctor?"

"Yes, he's over there," replied Death, pointing to a covered body upon one of the examination tables. The doctor walked over to the table, followed by Holmes and Watson. Holmes looked around the morgue and noticed what a strange place it was. The walls were whitewashed brickwork that hadn't been painted for several years. There were a few small windows set high in the walls, each of which had green painted frames. The ground was cobbled stone that had been covered with sawdust.

Upon reaching the body, Dr. Death lowered the shroud down to the waist of the headless figure. The blue-white skin showed signs of bruising around the shoulders and chest.

Holmes couldn't help noticing the similarity between the smell of the morgue and that of a butcher's shop. In addition to the familiar smell of a butcher's shop, there was also a strong smell of antiseptic.

"What can you tell me about the victim, Death?" asked Holmes, unable to resist smiling at his use of the word 'death'.

Chapter 2

"Well, his head has been removed," smiled the doctor, in reply. "Judging by the bruises on his shoulders and, more especially, the chest, I would say that he was held down whilst lying on his back during the attack. The last thing he possibly saw was the murder weapon speeding towards him."

Dr. Death paused shaking his head. Despite his many years in this profession, he still found the evidence of human cruelty hard to accept.

He then continued, "I would estimate that death occurred approximately 36 to 48 hours ago. Judging from the cuts on his neck it's probable that he was struck with…"

"A meat cleaver, yes I know," interjected Holmes. "I briefly examined the body yesterday afternoon. Has the head been found?"

"No, Mr. Holmes," replied Dr. Death.

"My I take a closer look at the wounds on the neck, Dr. Death?" asked Holmes.

"Of course you can. If you look, you can see that it took two blows of the weapon to reach the spine. The spine, itself, appears to have been struck several times. I can't tell you much more until I perform an autopsy."

Holmes looked closely at the wounds, specifically interested in the angle and depth of the cut lines.

"Look here, Watson," he said over his shoulder. Watson approached and looked at where Holmes was pointing.

The Dark Reckoning

"What is it, old fellow?" he asked.

"Judging by the bruising on the chest and the angle of these cut lines, it is probable that the murderer is right-handed and, possibly, quite tall."

"What makes you think that?"

"From where we are standing, on the victim's left hand side, the lines caused by the blade slant downwards towards the opposite side of the neck, as I told you yesterday after I had first seen the body. Also, notice that each cut appears to go more deeply into the neck the further down you look. This is consistent of the arc the blade would travel if wielded by a right-handed person. I would further venture that the bruising on the chest was caused by the murderer's left hand pressing the victim down whilst he started to cut his head off."

"That makes good sense, Holmes" replied Watson, carefully examining the wounds. "You mentioned that the spine had been snapped. How can you be sure?"

"If you look here, you can see several marks in the spine made by the blade. The deepest penetration occurs at this point," explained Holmes, indicating the mark on the spine. "Below this, there is no such marking. It's simply a clean fracture that's far more likely to have been caused by the head being snapped off. Furthermore, the skin at the back of the neck appears to have been torn, rather than cut."

Chapter 2

Holmes turned to Dr. Death and said, "Thank you doctor. You've been far more helpful than you might imagine. If you find anything further, please contact me."

"Yes, of course, Mr. Holmes. Good day, gentlemen."

Holmes and Watson turned to leave, and, as they did so, Watson's cane hooked itself onto one of the shrouds covering another body. The shroud was pulled off to reveal a corpse that had suffered severe putrefaction. The look of pure horror upon Watson's face caused both Holmes and Death to smile at each other.

"I'm so sorry, Doctor!" blurted out Watson.

"That's quite alright, Dr Watson. No damage has been done, and I don't think the victim has any modesty left in her," answered the doctor, still smiling.

"Why is this young woman so decomposed?" asked Holmes.

"It is suspected that she was a prostitute, murdered in Soho. Nobody found her body until almost two weeks after she died," explained the doctor.

Watson, feeling somewhat embarrassed by his reaction to seeing the body, attempted to change the subject by asking, "What made you go into this particular line of medicine, Doctor?"

"Well, with a name like mine, I would never inspire a great deal of confidence in living patients," smiled Death.

The Dark Reckoning

Holmes and Watson left the morgue and returned to Baker Street. Upon their arrival, Holmes went to his desk and wrote a cheque instructing his bank to pay five pounds to the Salvation Army to help the poorer inhabitants of the city.

Watson stood, looking out of the window and suddenly announced, "Holmes, it looks as if Lestrade is going to pay us a visit."

"Yes, I rather thought he might."

"What makes you say that, old fellow?"

"I believe he is coming to tell us that the murder weapon has been found."

"Holmes! That's incredible! You can't *possibly* know that – it's impossible! In fact, I'll wager five shillings that you're wrong!"

Holmes looked up at Watson and flashed a quick smile. "I suggest you refrain from gambling your money, Watson. Why not give it to a charity instead?"

"Very well, if you are right about what Lestrade will tell us, I will give one crown to the Salvation Army!"

"Very well," laughed Holmes, finding humour in Watson's compulsion to gamble, even when the benefactor was a charity.

Chapter 2

There was a loud knock on the door. "Come in, it's not locked," called out Watson. The door swung open and Mrs. Hudson entered announcing Inspector Lestrade.

Holmes stood from the desk at which he had been sitting. "Come in, Lestrade," he said, as he walked across the room and shook the inspector's hand. He then went on, "Mrs. Hudson, would you be so kind as to make us a pot of tea?"

Mrs. Hudson nodded approvingly and left to make the tea. Holmes turned back to Lestrade and said, "Take your coat off and have a seat, Lestrade."

Lestrade sat on the sofa, whilst Holmes returned to the desk seat he had been occupying a few moments earlier, and turned it to face Lestrade. Watson sat in his favourite chair, keen to find out the purpose of Lestrade's visit.

The inspector gave a sigh of relief as he sat, since this was the first time he had done so all day, and it was now approaching 2:20pm, according to the clock on the mantle piece. Lestrade noticed that there was a peaceful atmosphere to the room; a halcyon tranquillity that he found most welcoming. He looked around and noted that it hadn't changed much since his last visit. Books were still scattered everywhere. Despite that, the overall appearance of the room was tidy – probably due to Mrs. Hudson's constant attempts to tidy up after Holmes.

"What can the good doctor and I do for you, Lestrade?" asked Holmes.

"Well, Holmes…"

The Dark Reckoning

There was a rap on the door, so Watson went and opened it. Mrs. Hudson was standing outside with a tray. She smiled at the doctor, as he thanked her for the tea and took the tray she was carrying. She closed the door as Watson set the tray down on the table, poured three cups of tea and handed them out.

"Please, go on Lestrade. You were about to tell us something," said Watson, returning to his chair.

"We believe we've found the murder weapon!" There was a triumphant tone evident in the inspector's voice.

"Really!" exclaimed Holmes, smiling mockingly at Watson, who sat looking both confused and amazed that Holmes had known this was going to happen.

Watson turned to the inspector and asked, "Where was it, Lestrade?"

"We found it in Hyde Park, in some bushes about 50 yards from where the body was discovered."

"Is the weapon a meat cleaver, as suspected?" added Watson

"Yes, it's a meat cleaver alright. It looks to be new, or very nearly new."

A sudden idea came to Watson, prompting him to ask another question, "Are you able to say where this meat cleaver was purchased?"

Chapter 2

"Yes, it was sold by a shop called Smiths, located in Coventry Street. It's still got the price label on it. We've asked the staff at Smiths if anyone could remember who it was sold to. Nobody was sure, but one of them, remembered a man with dark hair, who was tall and of medium build, that purchased a cleaver last week. There was something about this man that seemed a bit sinister, apparently. Oh, and he had a Cockney accent. I don't think this information will be of much use to us as..."

"May we see it now, Lestrade?" interjected Holmes.

"How do you know I have it here?"

"The way in which you have been fiddling with that box suggests you are keen to display its contents to us."

Lestrade opened the box to reveal the blood-stained instrument.

"May I?" asked Holmes, indicating that he wished to handle the weapon.

"By all means, Holmes," replied the inspector.

Holmes took the weapon and looked at the blood, now dried, on the blade. Two very faint lines of dried blood were visible, confirming that two cuts had occurred, each having travelled further into the neck. The edge of the blade was blunted and deformed, possibly where it had struck the spine several times. There was also blood on the handle, which could have belonged to the murderer, as it was close to a splinter in the wood.

The Dark Reckoning

"I find it odd that the price label was left on the weapon," remarked Holmes, thoughtfully, as he continued to examine the meat cleaver. "Our murderer may have a cut and, possibly, a splinter in the palm of his right hand," stated Holmes, still looking closely at the weapon.

"How do you know that?" questioned Lestrade.

"If you look here, Inspector, you will see blood around this splinter. Furthermore, a fragment of the splinter is missing."

"I see," acknowledged Lestrade, whilst examining the handle. After they had finished examining the meat cleaver, Holmes told Lestrade everything he knew of the case. Although Lestrade tried to reciprocate, Holmes and Watson learned very little from the inspector. One thing he did add, was that the wife of Sir Charles Grey had confirmed the belongings found on the body were those of her husband. She had also confirmed that a birth mark found on the body matched her husband's.

After the inspector had left, Watson asked, "Who do you think is behind all this, Holmes?"

"It is impossible to say at present, old fellow, but I am sure that I have been manipulated into becoming involved. Somebody wants me to investigate, perhaps a villain reaping his, or her, revenge. In any case, we are currently left with little choice but to find out more about the murderer. So, let us go to Smiths and see if we are able to secure a more accurate description of the person that they thought sinister."

Chapter 2

As the two men left the apartment, Watson asked, "You indicated that the murderer might be a woman or a man, Holmes. I thought we had already established that it *must* be a man due to the strength needed to carry out the attack. Why have you not ruled a woman out?"

"It was most likely a man that actually committed the murder, due to the strength required to produce such deep cuts with the meat cleaver. However, we do not yet know who is orchestrating everything we have seen thus far. For all we know, somebody else could be behind all of this, Watson. The actual murderer may be nothing more than a henchman."

Upon arrival at Smiths, Holmes and Watson found the man behind the counter reluctant to speak about the mysterious man who had purchased a meat cleaver the previous week. A shilling soon loosened his tongue, however. He told them the man was not local – at least not known by anyone in the shop. He was clean-shaven, tidily dressed, although not very smartly, and his cockney accent had sounded false.

The two men returned to Baker Street. Watson, looking very perplexed, suddenly turned to Holmes and said, "I cannot wait any longer Holmes! How did you know that Lestrade had come to inform us that the murder weapon had been found?"

"Elementary, my dear Watson," smiled Holmes, "I saw something in the bushes in Hyde Park yesterday that I reported to a nearby officer. The police recovered it and found it to be the murder weapon. I arranged with Lestrade to bring it here today so that I could examine it.

The Dark Reckoning

I realise that I omitted to reveal these details to you, but I thought it would be more fun this way."

"Well confound it, Holmes!" shouted Watson, his face looking red and angry. "How could you let me bet on something that you already knew the outcome of? It's just *not* on, old chap!"

Holmes laughed and replied, "Come now, Watson. I did not take your bet but, instead, suggested you make a donation to charity."

Chapter 3

Chapter 3

The fog slowly swirled around the streets of London.

A note was delivered…

A clock struck eleven times, its sound muffled in the fog, as a subdued figure stepped out of a carriage. The figure walked along Haymarket, turned into a side turning and disappeared into the night.

The Dark Reckoning

She smiled, as she bid her colleagues goodnight and walked towards the exit. She liked working at The Theatre Royal, Haymarket and, although she only played a minor role, she knew that, one day, she would be a star. At twenty-one years of age, her youthful enthusiasm and pretty appearance stood her in good stead to realise that ambition.

The light above the exit illuminated her attractive face. Her skin was silky smooth and her eyes were deep blue and bright. She had full lips, a small nose and long blonde hair. She attracted many suitors, due to her natural beauty. Her hair cascaded over her shoulders and swung freely as she hurriedly walked away from the theatre. The sound of her footsteps cut through the fog and, from a distance, was the only evidence of her presence.

She looked behind her to confirm a suspicion that, in this haze, she would no longer be able to see the theatre; normally perfectly clear from this distance. All she could now discern of the theatre were diffused lights.

She passed under a streetlight, its glow illuminating the mist surrounding it. A shadow crossed her face as she passed under the light. She noticed that everything seemed so quiet within veil of fog surrounding her – as though nothing existed beyond the fifty, or so, yards that she could see.

The fog enhanced a feeling of mystery within her, an atmospheric dreamland in her heightened imagination. In this fantasy a great adventure, fraught with danger and excitement was about to take place, in which she played the principal role. She imagined herself in peril and being

Chapter 3

rescued by a handsome hero. A passing carriage, pulled by two horses, brought her abruptly back to reality; thus shattering the romantic mystery.

She continued along her usual route to Charing Cross Road by turning right into Orange Street, which served as a shortcut. This narrow street was cobbled with a small pavement on each side. The cobbles were uneven, an interminable mass of raised stones interspersed with mud filled pot holes. A row of buildings ran down both sides of the road, their rooftops barely visible in the freezing foggy air.

She turned left into Whitcomb Street, which disappeared into a misty oblivion, prompting a memory deep in the girl's subconscious to be recalled. It was so long ago, when she was just a young girl, but old enough to understand the horror before her eyes. Perhaps the atmosphere created by the fog was similar to that from the night of this memory. She shuddered at the recollection of the unclear images of her nightmares. 'Why should I remember now the evil I've fought so hard to forget?' she thought to herself. She shuddered as she recalled strange, distorted memories from the night she witnessed a man kill another.

She knew the killer to be dead, having been hanged for the murder she had witnessed. It was her evidence that condemned him to his fate, so she *knew* he was dead. Even so, she suddenly felt uneasy about what may lurk ahead in the eerie gloom. Her trepidation caused her to momentarily slow down. She inwardly laughed her unfounded fear away and continued her journey, albeit with a little more stealth in her step.

The Dark Reckoning

The flare of a match, as it lit a cigarette, briefly illuminated a man's pitted face, revealing a small scar on the right cheek. He rubbed his hands together in a futile attempt to defeat the cold night air. The man waited in a side street between Haymarket and Shaftesbury Avenue, drawing hard on his cigarette to calm his nerves.

In the distance he heard something… He strained his ears. Someone was approaching. He took the cigarette from his mouth, dropped it on the pavement and stepped on it. He held his breath in order to listen more closely. Someone *was* approaching. He found a house with no lights showing from within and crept into the small front garden. He squatted down behind the garden's wall and hid…

Holmes searched through file after file, read newspaper articles and accounts of old cases painstakingly written by Watson, several of which were somewhat embellished. His search became increasingly more frantic as his frustration grew.

"What does it mean?" he growled to himself. 'The answer must lie somewhere within these files,' he thought. He continued searching, scattering papers all over the room, becoming more agitated as he did so. Something within him knew that he held the answer he was so desperate to find, but he just could not find it. He

Chapter 3

searched through everything, but to no avail. He threw the last file across the room in anger. His gaze fell upon a small bottle and a syringe on the desk...

The girl continued along Whitcomb Street and then turned right into Lisle Street, which was silent and deserted. The only evidence of any people were the faint lights emanating from the windows of houses running along each side of the road. The gas streetlights lit areas along the street, whilst leaving other areas in invulnerable darkness. She walked into a dark shadow and then into the pale light offered by a streetlight.

She heard a sound come from a side street, as she passed by. She turned to face the direction of the sound, but could see only fog hanging densely in the night air. 'Must have been a cat, or something,' she reassuringly thought to herself; but the sound had unnerved her. Her heart beat faster than usual for a short while as she continued walking, nervously listening for any sounds coming from behind. Everything was silent, except for the distant sounds from the busier streets, so she breathed a sigh of relief.

The silence was suddenly broken and her heart began to pound in her chest once more, as a fresh feeling of fear gripped her. There were footsteps behind her where, moments before, there had been silence. She tried to calm herself by thinking, 'It doesn't matter that someone is walking behind. It's probably somebody that has come out of a house'. The pace of the footsteps quickened and

The Dark Reckoning

she began to panic, finding it hard to breathe continuously. The footsteps drew nearer and nearer until they sounded as though they were only a few yards behind her.

Her pace quickened in an attempt to evade whoever was following her. The footsteps behind did not increase in speed and, to her relief, she gained some distance between herself and those menacing footsteps. The street seemed much longer than usual to her. Why was there nobody else about? She thought of knocking on the front door of one of the houses to seek refuge, but dismissed the idea as foolish.

The footsteps seemed further back now. Her heart began to beat a little more easily and her breathing had returned to normal. She wondered why she had been so frightened, as she wasn't, by nature, easily scared. Perhaps it was the atmosphere created by the fog that reminded her of that terrible night, so many years ago.

Ahead, she could begin to make out the hazy lights in Charing Cross Road. There would be more people there, so she would be safe. Those lights looked so welcoming and she felt a great deal of relief as she approached them. But then the footsteps behind started to get closer again...

The pursuer rapidly gained on her. The thought occurred to the girl that it could be someone who had just realised they were late for an appointment. Perhaps the person would speedily pass her in a few moments.

She wanted to turn and confront her pursuer, but was too frightened and could not will herself to look behind.

Chapter 3

Something seemed wrong about the sound of these footsteps. The street became a sinister place, beckoning all of her deepest fears; just like that dreadful night so long ago. Her mouth was dry and she found it hard to swallow as, still, the footsteps drew nearer. She began to feel sick and felt her back and neck tingle as she sensed someone very close behind. Her heart was pounding heavily once again. She walked as quickly as she was able, perhaps trying to escape the feeling of impending danger, as well as whoever was so close behind.

Each step thundered in her ears. She wanted to run, but reasoned that the person would soon pass her by. She felt the person's presence only a few feet away from her. Her body was shaking violently, as every nerve sensed something evil behind her. Her breathing was fast and shivering, along with the rest of her body. No matter how much she tried to reason with herself, she could not overcome the feeling that she was in real danger. She *knew* something was very wrong.

A few steps later, she felt the front of a shoe catch her heel. Panic overwhelmed her frightened soul, and she was about to scream and run when she heard a brief rustle of clothing followed by a deafening crash upon the top of her head, accompanied by an excruciating pain. Her head was forced violently down into her neck and she heard an ear-splitting whistle.

Her world became unreal; the street lights started to swirl around her and the buildings began to spin uncontrollably. She tried to scream but her voice seemed to be trapped inside her throat. She wanted to run, but her legs would

The Dark Reckoning

not move. Instead they seemed to buckle and twist under the weight of her body and she just swayed to and fro.

A further flash of agonising pain forced her delirious body downwards. She saw the edge of the pavement rushing towards her and was aware of a loud snapping sound as her face smashed into the edge of the kerb. Her dazed vision saw blood upon the stony ground. The ground felt icy cold on her face as she lay, unable to move. The blood she could see around her began to seem further away and she no longer noticed the coldness. She didn't feel frightened anymore. Instead, she felt tranquil and serene as her fears vanished and her world gradually dissolved into blackness.

The man looked down at the girl laying half on the pavement and half in the gutter. Her body twitched as he looked at it. The wild excitement he felt showed in his crazed eyes, as he stood over his victim. A drop of blood fell from the head of the hammer he held, loosely, in his right hand.

He stood motionless, transfixed by the twitching body at his feet, until her heard a carriage approaching. He ran between two buildings, concealing himself in the shadows, as the sound of the horses hooves became louder.

The carriage came to a halt adjacent to the girl, who was no longer twitching. The man, upon recognising the four-wheeled Clarence carriage, came out of his hiding place

Chapter 3

and walked towards it. The driver stepped onto the pavement and opened the door. The two men then lifted the girl inside. The taller of the men, who had attacked the girl, climbed into the driver's seat, whilst the other got inside with the girl. The driver beckoned the horses to move and drove the carriage in the direction of Scotland Yard.

Inside the carriage, the man began to undress the girl. When she was naked, he took a saw and began to cut through her left arm, at the shoulder. The girl was lying on her back. The man noticed her distorted face as the carriage stopped under a streetlight. The force with which she had struck the kerb had broken her nose and jaw, and her skin was grazed and spattered with blood. Her bruised mouth was misaligned, with the bottom part of her jaw about an inch to the left of the top part. Her nose, dribbling blood, had been forced over to the left side of her face. There was a deep red mark running down the right side of her face that extended down over her right breast, where she had hit the edge of the kerb when she fell.

He continued sawing her left arm off, when her eyes suddenly opened and her right arm lashed out at him, badly scratching his face. He recoiled violently at the shock and pain of the sudden attack. In response, he stood and stamped on her throat. Her mouth opened and emitted a faint gurgle, but her eyes remained open, staring at him.

He took his walking cane and, still with his foot on her throat, thrust the pointed end into her left eye, forcing the eyeball to move sideways in its socket. He pulled the

The Dark Reckoning

cane out and then thrust it down once more into her eye. This time the end of the cane tore into her brain, damaging it too much to support life. Her body jerked and twitched for a few moments and then became perfectly still. As he removed his boot from her throat, a gush of blood spewed from her lifeless lips. He completed the task of cutting off her left arm, and then dressed her.

The carriage continued on its journey to Whitehall, and drew to a halt in amongst some shadows, near to Scotland Yard. The two men waited until the street was quiet, and then quickly dragged the dead body of the girl from the carriage and left her under an archway.

The larger of the men walked off, whilst the other returned to the carriage and began to consider his next move. He smiled, inwardly, with the knowledge that others were finally starting to pay for what they had done.

He climbed into the driver's seat and beckoned the horses to move. The carriage vanished into the night, merging with the darkness, as the fog slowly swirled around the streets of London.

Chapter 4

Chapter 4

In a quiet street, called Lisle Street, a hammer laid covered by frost. It had been accidently dropped in a moment of excitement and fear…

The past became the present as a man with wings flew away, eluding, once more, a man with a giant net. The net fell from the man's grip and he found himself in a warehouse filled with the limbs of dead bodies. Various tools were scattered around, such as screwdrivers, saws and hammers. The place was full of boxes, none of which

The Dark Reckoning

would open. Some boxes were stacked on top of each other, towering over the man, who was Holmes.

Holmes walked through the passageways formed between the towering boxes, and found himself in front of a set of giant interlocking cog wheels, slowly turning like those of a massive clock. As he approached, the wheels ceased turning.

The warehouse vanished and Holmes found himself running along an alley, but when he looked to his side, he saw that he was not moving. He stopped running, shouted, and closed his eyes. When his eyes reopened he was looking at a sign that read, 'J. J. Smith'. Bemused, he looked up at the large, ugly building the sign was fixed upon. Its dirty walls were dotted with numerous filthy windows. The roof looked like the serrated edge of a saw with its repeating peaks. The words 'Paul's Wharf' were written boldly in black letters on a strip of the wall that had been whitewashed.

Below, wreckages of small boats lay upon the muddy bed of the Thames. The tide was out and the water of the river ran like a narrow ribbon along the middle of the river bed.

Somehow, Holmes was now contemplating a narrow flight of steps that descended from Upper Swandam Lane. He began to walk down the steps and was confronted by a large, heavy door. Cautiously, he opened the door and walked through into a long room, which had a low ceiling. The ceiling had black painted wooden beams running across it. At the far end was another door, only just visible through the smoke that filled the room.

Chapter 4

Holmes did not venture far into the room. He looked around the dingy, smoky atmosphere and saw several inhabitants sitting or lying idle, the curse of this opium den having claimed their souls.

The door at the far end of the room was opened, and a dead body dragged out. As he stared towards the door, its surrounding walls became transparent so that he could see two men drag the body to the water's edge and throw it into the river. The Thames had acquired yet another secret to keep.

As the two men returned and closed the door, the thick, brown opium smoke manifested itself into the form of a faceless figure. The figure became a man with wings, but, suddenly, he vanished through the door at the far end of the room. Once again the man with wings had evaded Holmes.

Holmes gave chase and saw a young girl ahead clip one of the man's wings, slightly damaging it. Two policemen appeared and managed to trip the man, but he quickly got back up and took off into the air.

Holmes found the net in his hands again and was running with Watson, chasing the flying man who flew just above them, slightly out of reach. Holmes jumped and, this time, caught the man in his net. Both Holmes and Watson looked at the man, now tangled and writhing around in the net. A face formed upon the figure...

The Dark Reckoning

A judge was building the Houses of Parliament, and then a rope tightened…

The confused dreams remained with Holmes, as he gradually regained consciousness. As the potent cocktail of hallucinogenic drugs slowly wore off he knew, from his strange dreams, why Sir Charles Grey was dead.

Chapter 5

Chapter 5

"I do wish you would refrain from using drugs, Holmes," said Watson, with a worried look upon his face.

"Do stop moaning, Watson! I hadn't touched any drugs for months, prior to last night."

Mrs. Hudson arrived with the breakfast and morning papers, noticing the disarray in the room. She shook her head disapprovingly at the mass of the files, books and folders scattered everywhere, but said nothing. She had heard the commotion the previous evening and knew Holmes would have been desperately searching for something.

The Dark Reckoning

The two men sat at the table to eat. Holmes checked the date on the first newspaper he picked up, to find that it was Friday 9th December. His mind was still somewhat disoriented from the drugs he had taken the previous night. Flicking through the papers, he discovered an article that he had been hoping to find under the headline, 'Grey Day in Parliament'.

"I say, Watson, look at this headline. It's in rather bad taste, as the article describes the death of Sir Charles Grey."

"Why do you purchase such papers, Holmes, if they offend you so much?"

"I like to obtain as much information as possible. Although newspapers, such as The Times, provide good accounts, the views of the journalists that write the articles usually have a certain bias. Also, no single source of information contains all pertinent facts. Less serious papers often reveal information missing from the others."

Holmes read through every article he could find on Sir Charles Grey as he ate his breakfast. Most articles were more concerned with the political ramifications, rather than with details of the murder. All Holmes discovered was that the post-mortem had revealed nothing he didn't already know. Holmes decided to visit Dr. Death at the mortuary later that day to get a first hand account.

The men finished their breakfasts in silence. Holmes looked at the files lying all over the room that he had abandoned the previous night.

Chapter 5

He turned to Watson and said, "I had the strangest dream last night."

"I'm not surprised, considering the narcotics you took."

"Yes, I know, Watson! Please refrain from lecturing me! Anyhow, the dream has provided me with a clue. I now know where to look amongst these files." Holmes waved his hand, loosely pointing at the files scattered throughout the room. His eyes scanned the room as he searched for the file that had been revealed to him in the dream. Suddenly, his face lit up as he recognised the file he was seeking on the floor. Holmes obtained the information he sought, from the file, with a triumphant smile upon his face.

Watson shook his head in disbelief and asked, "How can a dream lead you to a clue in a murder investigation?"

"If my dream is to be believed, which I think it is; then someone is taking revenge for the execution of the murderer described in this file." Holmes held the file up towards Watson and then went on to tell him about the dream, including how he had chased the man with wings, the body that was dumped in the river from the opium den and the girl that had clipped the flying man's wings.

Watson was completely confused and asked, "What on earth can you deduce from all that nonsense?"

"Oh do come along, Watson!" exclaimed Holmes, taking a book that Watson was toying with and gently hitting him on the head with it. Watson looked shocked, as

The Dark Reckoning

Holmes laughed because of the sound the book made as it hit his head.

Watson became angrier as Holmes continued to laugh, and suddenly shouted, "That was jolly bad form, Holmes!"

"I'm sorry, old man," giggled Holmes. "The book made such a funny thud as it hit you on the head. It was very amusing, but I should not have hit you with it."

"I should hope that you are sorry! It's a bit much, you know – bopping a fellow's book on his head!"

"I have already apologized, Watson. Tell me, how would you describe the book?"

"It's bloody heavy!"

Watson's quick response caused both men to laugh. When they had composed themselves, Holmes continued, "Come along, Watson. It has been three days since the murder of Sir Charles Grey, so we must get to work."

"But today is Friday, Holmes, and Sir Charles was found on Wednesday. That's only two days."

"He was discovered on Wednesday, but murdered on Tuesday, according to what we were told by Dr. Death."

"Yes, of course. How silly of me. You were about to tell me of your dream. Perhaps, you could also explain why you've made such a mess with all these files."

Chapter 5

Holmes looked around the room and smiled, as he anticipated Mrs. Hudson's response to the prospect of cleaning up such disarray.

He then looked at Watson and said, "There is something about the events that have transpired, which leads me to believe this is all connected to an old case. I was searching for clues, but found only frustration, hence the mess. Now, let us analyse my dream."

"Very well, old fellow. But I'm afraid that you'll have to begin as I can't make any sense of what you've told me so far."

"Watson, I never expected anything else," smiled Holmes, jokingly. "My first thought is that the man with wings represents a criminal. Furthermore, I believe myself to be the man chasing him with the large net. The fact that he managed to evade me on several occasions, despite my attempts to capture him, has great significance."

"Yes, I think I understand. Perhaps you were trying to prove the criminal's guilt in some case, but he was able to escape justice as you were unable to provide enough evidence to have him convicted."

"Bravo, Watson!" exclaimed Holmes, delighting in his colleague's interpretation. "Your reasoning matches mine precisely. Let us continue. The large warehouse containing various limbs illustrates that the man with wings was most likely a murderer. Moreover, he was a serial killer, and carried out his crimes over a relatively small area."

The Dark Reckoning

"I can see how the limbs imply the man to be a serial killer, but how do you deduce that he confined his crimes to a small area?"

"Oh, that's quite simple to explain. The warehouse I found myself in represents his territory, and it wasn't very big in the dream. Furthermore, the warehouse contained many boxes that I perceived to be hidden clues. I knew that the clues were there, but were concealed from me, which is why I was unable to open the boxes in the dream."

"What about the giant interlocking wheels? What do they represent?" asked Watson, now completely intrigued.

Holmes laughed as he replied, "Ah yes, the wheels. They represented the wheels of justice. As I had not been able to provide enough evidence to secure a conviction, justice could not be served, and so the wheels stopped turning. Watson, I mentioned that I found myself running in an alley, but not achieving any movement. What do you make of that?"

"I think that it illustrates your frustration. You were trying to apprehend a killer by finding evidence against him. This is shown, in the dream, by your efforts to reach the end of the alley. As you were unable to produce sufficient evidence, your progress was hindered and so you were not moving anywhere, even though you were running. I think that when you stopped and shouted, you did so out of shear frustration, which led to you finding the clue you were so desperately seeking."

Chapter 5

"Yes, I concur," replied Holmes, "Except for the reason that I shouted. Don't forget that, as well as shouting, I also closed my eyes. I feel that the alley represents a particular line of investigation that I was pursuing. Upon realising that it was leading me nowhere, I stopped and shouted, as you mentioned, in frustration. I then discontinued this particular line of enquiry and so, in the dream, I closed my eyes. Upon opening my eyes, I saw the sign 'J. J. Smith'. This can be explained as me having found a new line of enquiry to my investigation."

Watson smiled, whilst shaking his head. "Holmes, you never cease to impress me with your ability to make such connections. I would never have attached any significance to you closing your eyes."

"Everything in the dream has significance, Watson."

Holmes poured himself some water and took a sip, as he continued, "The sign 'J. J. Smith' is on the side of Paul's Wharf, facing the river. As you may, or may not, be aware, this building is on the north bank of the Thames, in Blackfriars. In fact, it is just a stone's throw to the east of Blackfriars Bridge. I remember going there to catch the murderer."

"Are you saying that this sign has no symbolic meaning, Holmes?"

"Indeed. This is one part of my dream that adheres to the actual course of events. I vividly recall Paul's Wharf. I first encountered it from the south bank of the Thames, and was immediately struck by what an ugly building it was. The tide was low, revealing the rotting timbers of

The Dark Reckoning

old boats, embedded in the mud. These rotting remains lying in front of the decaying edifice of the building compounded its ugliness. I crossed Blackfriars Bridge and ventured towards the wharf. I found an unlocked entrance and ventured inside, purely out of curiosity."

Holmes paused, causing Watson to prompt, "Go on, Holmes. What did you find inside?"

"The place was damp with the smell of the river. It appeared to have been unused for quite some time. I slowly advanced into the building, very carefully, due to the darkness. I could hear a lot of strange noises all around me. It was not until my eyes adjusted to the dim light that I discovered the source of these noises. Scurrying in and out of old boxes, rusting anchors and other debris, were rats. There must have been hundreds, as the entire place seemed to be crawling with them. At one stage, I thought the shock of seeing them all was about to render me unconscious."

Holmes watched, as Watson shuddered, and then continued, "I believe the only reason I remained conscious was the realisation that the rats would have crawled all over me, if I had fallen. I remember cursing myself for walking in so foolishly."

"How did you get out, Holmes?"

"I lit a match in the hope that it would cause the rats to run away from me. Instead, it simply caused the vermin to run in all directions, like a sea of vile creatures. I just had to slowly make my way back to the door I had used to

Chapter 5

enter. Eventually, I reached the door and, with a sigh of relief, made my way through it."

"So what happened next?" asked Watson, now utterly enthralled.

"I continued a short distance along Upper Swandam Lane, which incidentally, the wharf backs on to. It is a nasty little alley, Watson. The very fact of my presence in such a squalid place made me feel ill at ease. Anyhow, Paul's Wharf is a large warehouse that has been divided into two. An archway runs along the divide from Upper Swandam Lane to the river's edge. It runs like a long tunnel through the building. I walked into the archway, which was dark and imposing. Approximately thirty feet from the river, on the right, there is a set of steps leading down from the tunnel to a low black door. I carefully walked down the steps to the door."

"Was anyone with you? I shudder to think what may have become of you venturing into such a place on your own, Holmes."

"You are right, Watson, but that is exactly what I did. There was an oil lamp hanging above the door that burned dimly. I had disguised myself, so I decided to enter. I tried the door, which was not locked, so I opened it and went inside. The pungent aroma from within was overwhelming, Watson. This was the opium den from my dream. As I moved inside, the proprietor looked at me with disdain. I stood just inside the doorway for a moment, looking around the room."

The Dark Reckoning

Watson was shaking his head in disapproval. "Holmes, you could have been killed going to a place like that on your own."

"I agree that it was a foolish venture. In retrospect, I find it hard to believe I took such a course of action. The room was quite long and narrow. It had a low ceiling with several black support beams running across. There was a small bar to the left of the room, behind which stood the proprietor, still observing me with suspicion. The room was filled with addicts lying on the straw covered stone floor. The smell of vomit and urine was easily detectable, despite the smoky atmosphere. There were four gaslights on the walls, two on each side of the room. The glow emanating from the lights was highly diffused by the thick brown smoke."

"That sounds absolutely hideous, Holmes," commented Watson.

"It was, old fellow. It saddens me a great deal to think that those who sell these drugs profit from such suffering. Those poor wretches lying in that den slowly killed themselves as others made money from them. The smoke in the room was a refuge to the ghosts, nightmares and hell seen only through the eyes of those mesmerised souls. They just laid there like zombies, Watson."

"Why did you go there, Holmes?"

"I had learned that the man I suspected of the murders had been seen in the place on numerous occasions. I hoped to obtain some information about him but, as soon as I saw the place, I knew it was a worthless venture. None of the

Chapter 5

occupants were going to reveal anything to someone like me. The room was littered with rats, some dead, others scurrying over and around the addicts."

Holmes became quiet as he thought back to the opium den. He tried to think if he had witnessed something at the time and not realised it, but nothing came to mind.

Watson, seeing the perplexed look on Holmes' face, asked, "Is there anything else that you can tell me from your dream last night, Holmes?"

"Indeed, Watson. The next extract from my dream is another based on fact. In the dream, I was able to see through the wall at the far end of the opium den. I could see two men dumping a body into the river. What happened, in reality, was that one of the poor wretches had died of an overdose prior to my arrival. His body was being tied up in a sack by two men at the end of the room. The men dragged the dead body through the door and then returned."

"But you said that, in your dream, you saw them dump the body into the river. Did that not happen in reality?"

"I did not see, Watson. However, I am aware that, in many such establishments, dead bodies are put in weighted down sacks and hidden until after dark. With the cover of nightfall, the bodies are usually loaded into a boat and taken to a quiet location where the river is deep. There, they are tipped out of the boat and into the river, where they sink without a trace."

The Dark Reckoning

"So, your trip to the opium den was a dangerous waste of time," remarked Watson, somewhat scornfully.

"No, it proved to be very useful. Just after the two men returned, I was about to leave. However, I noticed the suspect exit through the same door that the two men had just entered. I decided to pursue the man and started into the den, stepping over the addicts as I went. Upon witnessing me move so quickly, the proprietor signalled the two men. They began to approach me with the intention of beating me senseless."

As Holmes paused, he could see the anticipation in Watson's face. "What happened next, Holmes?"

"I had little time to decide whether to run, or fight. I turned to make a retreat, but there were too many people obstructing my path. So, I turned and faced my opponents, having resolved to fight back, if attacked. Neither of the men attacked, however. Instead, they forced me to the end of the room and shoved me through the very door that I had intended to go through in pursuit of my suspect. This led to a smaller, but wider room that was completely empty, except for the sack containing the dead body. There was a pair of large doors at the end of the room that were slightly ajar, through which the suspect must have made his escape."

Holmes paused again and took a sip of his water. He beckoned to Watson, as if to ask if he would also like a glass, but Watson declined.

After taking another sip, Holmes continued, "One of the two men grabbed my arms from behind, whilst the other,

Chapter 5

standing in front of me, clenched his dirty fist. The man behind me managed to clasp my arms tightly behind my back, as the other man drew his fist back. He threw his fist forward with all his might. Somehow, I managed to twist and move my head to the side, so that the fist went crashing into the face of the man behind me."

Holmes paused again, took another sip of water and then continued, "The man behind me released his grip and fell to the ground, unconscious. The other man was so shocked by what had happened, he froze momentarily, giving me time to bunch my fist and hit his jaw as hard as I could. To my intense relief, he fell to the ground and did not get up. I left the building via the two doors, which opened out onto a small path next to the river. I searched the path in both directions, but found no sign of the suspect."

"Holmes, you were lucky to get out of there unscathed. You should *never* take such risks"

"You are quite right, Watson. I was foolish to go into such a place alone. Anyhow, let us continue analysing my dream."

"Oh yes, of course. What happened next, old fellow?"

Setting his glass down on the table, Holmes thought for a few moments, before proceeding, "The next part of the dream involved a small girl who managed to clip a wing of the man with wings. There were also two policemen who managed to trip him. All these people represent witnesses that I found during the course of my investigation."

The Dark Reckoning

"So, was anything here based on actual events that took place, Holmes?" asked Watson.

"No. The people did exist, but not the events I just described. I believe that each witness I found impaired the ability of my suspect to continue his murders. In the dream, this manifested itself as the witnesses physically impairing the criminal's progress. In reality, each witness supplied evidence that led to his conviction."

Watson was sitting on the edge of his seat, his eyes wide as he was unable to resist any longer. Suddenly, he asked, "Well, who was this man, Holmes? I mean the one with wings"

"In a moment, Watson," replied Holmes, relishing the knowledge that he was making his friend wait for the answer. He then went on, "Before I reveal his identity, there is something else to be learned from my dream. There was a part where you and I gave chase to the man, eventually trapping him in the large net. At this point, his face became clear, which represents me remembering his identity. The final part of the dream showed a judge building the Houses of Parliament. This represents Sir Charles Grey. Although he later went on to become a Member of Parliament, he was originally a judge. In actual fact, he was the judge that convicted the murderer, and sentenced him to death."

"Do you think that's why his head was cut off a few days ago, Holmes?"

Chapter 5

Holmes nodded in answer to Watson's question and waited for the next question, which he was sure would be asked soon. He didn't have to wait long.

"So, who was the criminal, Holmes?"

Holmes smiled and said, "Stanley Wood."

"Oh yes, I remember that case. But he can't be killing people as he was hanged."

"Yes, that is true, Watson. I believe that someone close to him is now avenging his death."

"But who could it be, Holmes?" asked Watson, desperation evident in his voice.

"I can't be sure at this time, Watson, but I suspect that it may be his brother. He went mad when Stanley was arrested for murder and had to be institutionalised. I believe he deteriorated further after Stanley was put to death. We can check to determine whether he is still in the asylum whilst we are at Scotland Yard."

"I remember reading about him in the newspapers. His name is Stephen. Do you know what he looks like, Holmes?"

"Yes, I interviewed him shortly after he was institutionalised. He stands approximately 5 feet, 9 inches and is of slim build, although it is possible that he has gained weight since I last saw him. His hair is light brown and he has a large, bulbous nose. He has particularly thick lips and his eyes seem too close together. They have a piercing look that clearly hints at his unhinged mind. If it is true that the eyes are the windows to the soul, Watson, then this man's soul is evil."

Chapter 6

Chapter 6

There was a knock on the door.

"Enter!" called Holmes.

Mrs. Hudson came in and handed Holmes a piece of paper. "This arrived for you yesterday evening, Mr. Holmes," she said, somewhat nervously. She half expected the delay in bringing the note to annoy Holmes.

Instead, he smiled and, in a calm voice, asked, "Why did you not deliver the note to me yesterday evening, when it arrived?"

"I... I forgot, Sir."

The Dark Reckoning

"Very well, Mrs. Hudson," responded Holmes. He noticed how nervous the housekeeper appeared, and added, "There is no need to be frightened. I imagine the noise I was making yesterday evening dissuaded you from bringing the note to me at the time."

"It did, Sir. I could hear lots of noise, and you shouting. I was scared to knock on the door! That's why I thought it best to say that I forgot to give the note to you."

"I understand. However, in future please bring all correspondence to me in a timely manner. Do not let us detain you, Mrs. Hudson." Holmes beckoned to the door, indicating that he wished her to leave. Mrs. Hudson gave a smile and quickly left the room.

Holmes unfolded the piece of paper and exclaimed, "Our messenger has sent us another message, Watson! And this one is somewhat more cryptic."

"What does it say?" enquired Watson, suddenly interested in the note Holmes was holding.

"It reads as follows. *'The final curtain falls and law is devoured.'* Somewhat obscure, don't you think, Watson..." Holmes' words seemed to trail off and a sudden look of despair adorned his face. He looked down at the floor for a few seconds and then back at Watson and gravely added, "Watson, I fear that three murders may have taken place last night."

"What do you *mean*? I don't understand how you can make such a claim!" replied Watson, clearly shocked and perplexed by what he had just heard.

Chapter 6

Holmes found the previous note that had been delivered a few days earlier, and handed both to Watson.

He gestured for Watson to look at the notes, and said, "As you can see, both of these notes were written by the same hand. If you look more closely, you will see that they are both written on the same type of paper. Although the author attempted to use two different forms of handwriting, there are unmistakable consistencies between the handwriting on each of the notes."

Watson studied both pieces of paper in his hand. "I can see the resemblances that you mention, but I fail to understand how these notes lead you to think that there were three murders committed last night."

"As we know, the first note was delivered in connection with the murder of Sir Charles Grey. It directed me to go to the Prince of Wales Gate in Hyde Park at 4:00pm on Wednesday 7th December, so that I should happen upon the politician's dead body."

"I'm sorry, old fellow, but I don't follow."

"You will recall that, when we were discussing the case of Stanley Wood, I mentioned three witnesses. One was a young girl and the other two were policemen. The girl, named Sally Spencer, grew up and became an actress. Does this mean anything to you yet, Watson?"

"Yes, it does!" exclaimed Watson, grimly, a horrified look showing on his face. He then went on, "In the note, '*the final curtain*' implies that Miss Spencer may be in danger. Furthermore, '*law is devoured*' can be associated

The Dark Reckoning

with the two policemen. What were their names, Holmes?"

"I don't recall." Holmes thought for a moment and then added, "I may have their names in a file. Hold on a moment, whilst I check." He searched through a stack of files on the desk and found the one he needed. He flicked through the pages within. "Ah, here we are. Their names are given here as P.C. Roach and P.C. Baxter."

"Are they still in the Police force, Holmes?"

"I don't know. We shall ask when we get to Scotland Yard."

There was a knock on the door. "It's unlocked, come in," called Holmes. Mrs. Hudson entered the room, followed by a young woman.

"This young lady wishes to speak with you, Mr. Holmes," said the housekeeper. "I tried to explain that you might be busy, but…"

"That is quite alright, Mrs. Hudson," interjected Holmes, having noticed the troubled expression on the girl's face. Judging by her appearance, Holmes thought her to be no older than about twenty years of age. "Of course I have time. Thank you, Mrs. Hudson," he smiled.

Mrs. Hudson left and closed the door behind her. The young lady shifted awkwardly on her feet and stared at the floor, only occasionally glancing up at the two men in the room.

Chapter 6

Watson smiled at her when she caught his eye, and asked, "May I take your coat, Miss?" The girl returned his smile, removed her coat and handed it to him. Watson hung it over a hat stand by the door.

"Would you care to sit by the fire and warm yourself?" Holmes asked the girl.

"Thank you, Sir," she replied, as she sat where Holmes had directed. Holmes sat in a chair opposite the girl, who was now looking around the room. She noticed the pale, delicately patterned wall paper, the pattern of which was only just discernable. She wondered whether this subtlety matched Holmes' taste, or whether he was not concerned with such matters. Several paintings hung on the walls, mostly small in size. Additionally, there were three swords fixed to one wall, one above another, in succession. Over the fireplace, behind the clock, was a large mirror. A gaslight was positioned on each side of the mirror, as well as another two on the opposite wall. Somehow the décor of the room made the girl feel more at ease.

"How may I be of help?" asked Holmes, looking at the distraught girl. She was very attractive and had smooth pale skin and dark brown hair. Her eyes were deep blue and looked as though she had recently been crying. Holmes guessed who she was, based on her resemblance to a picture of Sally Spencer that he had seen in the Times a few weeks beforehand.

"My name is Susan Spencer, Mr. Holmes. I've come to report a missing person, and would ask for your help in finding..."

The Dark Reckoning

"Her," finished Holmes. "You are referring to your sister, Sally Spencer, are you not?" he then asked.

"Well, yes! But how did you know that?"

"I saw a photograph of your sister in the Times a few weeks ago, in a review of the play she is currently appearing in. You have a close resemblance to her."

Holmes glanced over at Watson, still holding the two notes in his hands, and tried to conceal the awful feeling he had about the fate of the young lady's sister. He knew that Sally Spencer was the young witness who had helped to secure the conviction of Stanley Wood several years earlier. That, along with the reference to the '*final curtain*' in the note Watson was holding, led Holmes to believe that Sally was possibly now dead.

Susan Spencer was now warming her delicate, small hands by the fire. She observed Holmes quizzically, waiting for him to respond. He raised his right hand and placed his thumb under his chin and pointed his index finger up the side of his right cheek, as he said, "Tell me why you suspect your sister to be missing, Miss Spencer."

"She told me that she would visit after her performance had finished last night. Her intention was to stay the night. I didn't expect her to arrive until after eleven thirty, but she failed to turn up."

"Where do you live, Miss Spencer?" asked Holmes.

"28 Charing Cross Road, Mr Holmes."

Chapter 6

"Does your sister usually visit you after finishing work at the theatre?" enquired Watson.

"Yes, some evenings she does, and *always* on Thursdays."

Holmes confirmed something he already knew, by asking, "In which theatre does your sister currently work?"

"She is working at The Theatre Royal, Haymarket."

"How does she typically get from the theatre to your place of residence?"

Susan looked down at the floor as if embarrassed to admit what she was about to say, and quietly answered, "She walks, Mr. Holmes."

"Do you know by which route she travels when she visits you from the theatre, or, indeed, if she always uses the same route?"

"I'm not sure," replied Susan, shaking her head.

Holmes looked thoughtful, as he gently rubbed his index finger back and forth over his cheek.

After a few moments, he looked directly at Susan and said, "Tell me more about your suspicions, Miss Spencer."

"Yes, of course, Mr Holmes. As I mentioned, I didn't expect her to arrive until after eleven thirty. I don't know why, but I began to feel worried at about a quarter past eleven. I tried to dismiss the feeling as a silly emotion,

The Dark Reckoning

but it wouldn't go away. By the time my clock struck twelve, I was very worried." The girl's bottom lip began to tremble and her eyes filled with tears, as she relived her anguish.

"Try not to upset yourself, Miss Spencer," said Holmes in a soothing voice. He then turned to Watson and asked, "Watson, would you ask Mrs. Hudson to make us all a cup of tea?"

Susan smiled at the kindness shown by Holmes and a tear rolled down her cheek. "I'm sorry, gentlemen. I didn't mean to cry. It's just that I don't know what to do! I'm so worried about Sally."

Watson stood and gave the young lady a smile. "I shall arrange for tea to be sent up," he said, leaving the room.

As Watson left, Holmes asked, "Do you feel strong enough to continue, Miss Spencer?"

The girl, drying her eyes with a lace handkerchief, replied, "Yes, Mr. Holmes; but there's not much more to tell. I waited up all night. It was awful, and the hours dragged by. The later it got, the more my glimmers of hope turned to despair."

Do you live alone, Miss Spencer?"

"No, I share a house with two other girls. We all work at the Bank of England. My parents live in Devon, and I haven't lived with them for over two years."

"Is there anything else you can tell me?"

Chapter 6

"Only that I waited up all night, in case she arrived. When she didn't, I took a carriage to her place early this morning. She lives alone in Hanover Street, near Oxford Circus. I knocked, but there was no answer, so I let myself in. She wasn't there. I went to the nearest police station to report her missing, but was told that I would have to wait another day before they would file a report. The police officer I spoke to suggested that I might contact you in the meantime."

"I see. Do you have a recent photograph of your sister?"

"Yes, I do," smiled Susan, taking the photograph out of her bag and showing it to Holmes. "I thought it would be a good idea to take it to the police station."

"May I retain this photograph, until I have completed my investigation, Miss Spencer?"

"Of course you may, Mr. Holmes," replied Susan, handing the photograph to the detective.

Watson returned, carrying the tea. He poured out three cups and gave one to the young lady, one to Holmes and then sat down with his own. Holmes did not want to distress the girl any further by questioning her about her sister, so instead, he remarked, "You mentioned that your parents live in Devon, Miss Spencer. Dr. Watson visited Devon for a week, just over a month ago."

Susan looked over to Watson and smiled. She then asked, "Which part of Devon did you visit, Dr. Watson?"

The Dark Reckoning

"I stayed with a farmer friend in Paignton to help him on his farm. It was nice to get out of London for a break."

"My parents live quite close to Paignton, Dr. Watson. They are in Brixham. I haven't visited them since the summer."

"Both Holmes and I know Brixham well", added Watson.

"Have you known the farmer you stayed with for long, Doctor?" asked Susan, now appearing a little more composed and relaxed.

"Not particularly long. Holmes and I made the acquaintance of a certain Arthur Smith, just over six months ago. He recently acquired a small farm in Paignton, so I offered to go and help get him settled in. It was hard work, but made a very enjoyable change from life in London."

Susan smiled and remarked, "That was kind of you Dr. Watson." Suddenly, the thought of her missing sister returned to her mind and her smile vanished, to be replaced by an anguished expression.

Holmes noticed the girl's change of heart and said, "We will look into finding your sister today, Miss Spencer."

"Thank you, Mr. Holmes. I appreciate your help a great deal. I've taken up enough of your time, so will bid you farewell. If you need to contact me, I will be at 28 Charing Cross Road."

Chapter 6

"Very well, Miss Spencer. We will be in touch as soon as we discover anything," said Holmes, walking towards the door to retrieve the young lady's coat. He handed it to her and she put it on.

"Good bye, gentlemen," said Susan. Both men replied in kind to the girl. Holmes walked her to the front door and saw her out.

When Holmes returned to the room, Watson looked worried.

"What is it, Watson?" asked the detective.

"When I went to make the tea with Mrs. Hudson, it occurred to me that the clue in the note delivered last night could be referring to Sally Spencer's murder, and that she may already be dead."

"The same thought occurred to me, old man. I considered asking Miss Spencer about the murder trial where her sister had been a witness, but thought better of it. She seemed so distraught and I didn't wish to upset her unnecessarily"

"Perhaps you should have asked her anyway. By not doing so, you may have given her false hope."

"Yes, I realise that, Watson. However, I don't *know* for certain if Sally Spencer has come to any harm. There would be little point in making a statement that could cause such great anguish, before the facts are established. I felt that reminding Miss Spencer of the trial would only

The Dark Reckoning

give her another reason to think that something terrible has become of her sister."

Watson nodded his head in agreement, and sat back comfortably in his chair.

"Come along now, Watson! There isn't time for you to relax. We need to get to Scotland Yard."

Watson scowled at Holmes briefly, and stood up to get ready to leave.

Chapter 7

Chapter 7

It was a bitterly cold morning, fog hanging in the air and no hint of sunshine, made for a miserable atmosphere. Frost lay thick on the ground, as Holmes and Watson left 221b Baker Street and walked over to a waiting Hansom cab on the opposite side of the road.

Holmes approached the driver and asked, "Would you be so kind as to take us to Scotland Yard?"

"Yes, Sir, I'll take ya wherever ya wanno go," answered the cab driver. The two gentlemen climbed into the small carriage and the driver shook the reins, instructing the horse to move along.

The Dark Reckoning

Holmes rubbed his gloved hands together and remarked, "My word, Watson, it is bitingly cold this morning. I believe this freezing fog will be with us for the entire day. It's quite a contrast from yesterday morning when the sun shone so brightly."

"Yes, old fellow. I shall not complain if we are to get anymore mornings like yesterday during the course of the winter."

The two men made small talk until the carriage pulled up in Whitehall, opposite the archway leading to Scotland Yard. They noticed a crowd had assembled outside of the police station, so quickly disembarked from the carriage, after Holmes paid the driver.

Holmes turned to Watson and, with some urgency, beckoned, "Come, Watson!" as he started to run towards the crowd.

Holmes and Watson struggled to fight their way to the front of the crowd, where they found an area that had been cordoned off. Several police officers patrolled the area, preventing anyone from crossing the barrier.

Holmes caught the attention of one of the officers and said, "My name is Sherlock Holmes and it is *imperative* that I, and my associate, speak to Inspector Lestrade."

"Mr. Holmes, Sir!" exclaimed the officer, recognising the great detective. He lifted the tape and continued, "Step under, gentlemen. Inspector Lestrade is inside the station."

Chapter 7

"Thank you, Officer," acknowledged Holmes, as the two men stepped under the barrier. As they left the crowd, both men saw a pool of blood on the pavement under the archway. Holmes did not stop to look at the blood, which surprised Watson. Instead, he made his way straight to the police station.

As they approached the station, Holmes said, "I often find myself loathing peoples' fascination with death. Look at that crowd, their insatiable curiosity driving them to look at a pool of blood."

"You can't blame people for being curious, Holmes."

"You are right, Watson. I think my anger is directed more towards the fact that such crowds unwittingly obliterate vital evidence from crime scenes."

The two men turned into Scotland Yard, climbed the few steps to the entrance and went inside. The desk clerk informed them that Inspector Lestrade was in his office, and suggested that the two of them should go straight in. As they made their way to Lestrade's office, they met him walking towards them in a corridor.

"Mr. Holmes! Dr. Watson. Good morning to you both," said the Inspector.

Not acknowledging Lestrade's greeting, Holmes asked, "Lestrade, what happened under the archway?"

"We found the body of a young lady. She has been taken to the morgue. I am on my way there now to find out more. I saw her briefly before she was taken, but there

The Dark Reckoning

were too many people around. As the crowd was growing larger, and more curious, it was decided to move the body to the morgue as soon as possible. Would you gentlemen like to join me?"

"Very well," replied Holmes.

The three men left the station and walked to the morgue. On the way, Holmes took the photograph of Sally Spencer from his pocket.

"Is this the dead girl you found this morning?" he asked, showing the photograph to Lestrade.

Lestrade stopped, dead in his tracks, as he stared at the photograph.

He took time before replying, "I think that *is* her. I can't be completely sure though, as her face had been really smashed in. How did you know, or suspect, that she could be the victim?"

"I was visited by her sister this morning, who wished to report her missing. The police had referred her to me as it has been less than a day since her sister was last seen. Prior to her visit, Watson and I had been discussing the case of Stanley Wood, who was hanged for murder. The young lady in that photograph was a witness at his trial, and I fear somebody may have killed her in a revenge attack."

"That's impossible! It's a ridiculous assumption to make, Holmes. What evidence do you have?" asked Lestrade in a cold tone, whilst shaking his head.

Chapter 7

"Would you still think it so ridiculous if you learned that Sir Charles Grey was the judge that sentenced Stanley Wood?"

"Errrm. I... errrm don't know. No! That *still* doesn't prove anything!" retorted the policeman.

Holmes smiled, as Watson retrieved the two notes from his pocket and handed them to Lestrade, adding, "Look at these, Inspector."

Lestrade looked at the notes, with a puzzled expression. He didn't say anything, but looked up quizzically at Holmes.

Holmes took the notes from him and explained, "These were delivered to me on separate occasions. This note was delivered a few days ago, and is how I happened to be near Hyde Park when Sir Charles Grey's body was there. The other note was left last night. I believe the two to be connected, as the hand writing shows signs of being written by the same person. The reference in the note to the '*final curtain*' could refer to someone in the theatre. If I am correct about the identity of the dead girl, she was the actress, Sally Spencer."

"Well, that does make sense," said Lestrade, now beginning to see how Holmes had arrived at his hypothesis. "What about the other part of the note, where it mentions something about the law being devoured?"

"There were three witnesses whose evidence resulted in Wood's execution. One was the girl I have already spoken of, and the other two were policemen. Their

The Dark Reckoning

names were P.C. Baxter and P.C. Roach. If I am correct about the meaning behind this note, these men are either in grave danger, or already dead."

"Let us pray that you are wrong, Holmes. I know both of them. They are based at Scotland Yard. P.C. Baxter is now a sergeant, having been promoted a couple of years ago," replied the Inspector. He stood stroking his chin for a moment and then asked, "If Stanley Wood was executed all those years ago, why is someone avenging his death now?"

It was Watson that answered the question, "Stanley Wood had a brother, called Stephen, who went mad and was committed to an asylum after his brother was put to death."

"So, you think he is the killer of this girl and Sir Charles Grey? How can he be, if he is locked up in an asylum?"

Holmes smiled briefly and said, "You have serendipitously stumbled upon the reason for our visit, Lestrade. We wanted to find out whether Stephen Wood has escaped, or been released from the asylum. With all the commotion, I forgot to ask you, whilst we were at Scotland Yard."

"We may as well go back to the station and find out before we head off to the morgue, gentlemen" suggested Lestrade. "Do you know the name of the asylum that he was put in?"

"It was The Middlesex County Lunatic Asylum," answered Holmes.

Chapter 7

The men returned to Scotland Yard. Lestrade left Holmes and Watson, and went to make enquires about Stephen Wood. After a short while, he returned with a case file.

"It looks like you might be onto something, Holmes. Stephen Wood was released from Middlesex County Lunatic Asylum six months ago. An entry was made in our case file, stating that the asylum considered him completely sane." Lestrade showed Holmes the case file, which didn't contain very much information.

"Six months ago," repeated Holmes, thoughtfully, as he looked through the case file.

"Holmes, you described this man as evil. It seems implausible that such a character could ever be completely cured of his insanity," commented Watson.

"Indeed," replied Holmes. "I'll venture that he managed to convince staff at the asylum of his sanity. I found him to be an *extremely* adept liar, when I questioned him in the case of his brother. I doubt whether he was truly rehabilitated, at all." Holmes handed the case file to Lestrade, who gave it to the desk sergeant, asking him to file it away.

The three men left the police station, and started walking to the morgue.

On the way, Holmes asked, "What can you tell me about the girl at the morgue, Lestrade?"

"Well, as I said, her face has been smashed in very badly. One of her eyes has been pushed into her head. Also, her

The Dark Reckoning

hair was matted with blood at the back, where she appears to have been hit with something. The worst thing though, is that her left arm has been cut off, and is missing."

A young police constable left Scotland Yard and ran along the road, calling after Inspector Lestrade. The Inspector turned and asked, "What is it, officer?"

"Sir," panted the young policeman. "We just received a report that two police officers were murdered last night!"

"Are their identities known?" asked Holmes.

"Yes Sir. They were P.C Roach and Sergeant Baxter. They worked in Scotland Yard. Everyone knew them!" exclaimed the young officer, the shock of hearing the news clearly evident on his face.

Lestrade looked visibly staggered. It took him some time, before he answered the young officer. "I have to go to the morgue now, but I want to hear everything about these murders when I return. Go back to the station and tell the Chief Inspector that I will come and see him, as soon as I return from the morgue. Do you understand, Officer?"

"Of course, Sir," answered the young officer, turning to go back to Scotland Yard.

Holmes called after the young policeman, "Do you know where their bodies are, Officer?"

"I don't know, Mr. Holmes," replied the young policeman, suggesting, "They may already be at the morgue."

Chapter 7

Lestrade turned to Holmes. He shook his head, in disbelief, as he said, "Holmes, it really is beginning to look like Stephen Wood may be our killer. Do you agree?"

"I concur, up to a point, Lestrade. All we have, at this point in time, is circumstantial evidence. It is possible that someone else is carrying out the murders, with the intention of using Wood as a scapegoat."

The men entered the morgue and, after exchanging pleasantries, Dr. Death confirmed that the two policemen had been delivered earlier that morning. He showed the men all three corpses. A horrified expression appeared on Lestrade's face, as he recognised the dead bodies of the two policemen. He stumbled slightly and steadied himself against the wall.

"Lestrade, are you alright?" asked Watson, going to the Inspector's assistance.

"I'm sorry," replied Lestrade. "These two are Sergeant Baxter and P.C Roach. I wasn't expecting to see anything like this."

"Would you like to sit down for a moment, Inspector?" asked Dr. Death.

"No, I'm alright. I've seen enough dead bodies. It's just a shock when you see people that you know."

Holmes looked at Dr. Death and asked, "May I examine the girl's body, Doctor?"

The Dark Reckoning

"Yes, Mr. Holmes, of course you may."

Of the three corpses, the girl had been mutilated the most. Her face was smashed in and she had a long bruise that ran from her forehead, down across her chest and stomach and ending on the top of her thigh. Her left arm was missing. The point at which it had been cut appeared slightly rough and very straight, leading Holmes to suspect that it had been cut off with a saw.

Holmes looked at where the girl's eye had been pushed in. Immediately below her left eye was a deep round puncture, approximately a half-inch in diameter. This appeared to be one of two blows, as the same circular puncture was visible in her eye socket.

Watson stood next to Holmes, looking at the girl's face. "What do you think did that to her face? Her nose and the bottom half of her jaw have been pushed so far to the left. What could *do* such a thing?"

Holmes turned to Watson, and replied, "Judging by the damage to her face, as well as the long bruise running down the upper half of her body, I think she may have hit the edge of a roadside kerb when she fell. If so, the force of the impact may have misaligned her nose and jaw to such an extent."

"There is more evidence that supports that theory, Mr. Holmes," added Dr. Death. "She was hit twice on the head, from behind." The doctor turned the girl's head to reveal an area that he had shaved. "As you can see from the shape of these wounds, it appears that she was hit with something like a hammer. The force of each blow was

Chapter 7

extreme, as I can feel that her parietal bone has been broken."

"Did these blows kill her, Dr. Death?" asked Holmes.

"It is possible, but I'm not convinced that they did."

Holmes lifted the girl's right hand and, taking a magnifying glass from his pocket, began to examine it closely. "There is some skin under three of her fingernails. I believe she may have scratched one of her attackers."

"How many attackers were there?" asked Lestrade, with a slight hint of sarcasm, as he felt that Holmes could not possibly know the answer to that question.

Holmes smiled wryly at the inspector, and explained, "It is my suspicion that two men were involved, the same two men the tramp described to me following the murder of Sir Charles Grey. Based on his description, one of these men is large. This man must also be especially strong if he cut the head of Sir Charles Grey off. As we know, it took but a few blows of the cleaver to cut through to the spine before the head was snapped off."

Lestrade looked puzzled and said, "I don't know quite what you are getting at, Holmes."

"As the doctor just explained, Sally Spencer was hit twice from behind and suffered damage to her parietal bone. This suggests that her attacker was significantly taller than she was and very strong; possibly the larger of the two men the tramp told me of."

The Dark Reckoning

"I see. That makes sense. But how do you know there was another man involved in *this* particular murder?"

"I am not absolutely certain there was, Lestrade. I can only present conjecture based upon the facts at hand. At this stage, it helps to visualise a possible sequence of events, in order to form a theory. More evidence is required to prove, or disprove, this theory, however. Shall I continue?"

"Please do," added the inspector, trying not to show that he was impressed with the way that Holmes' mind could make such connections.

"The second man that the tramp spoke of, the well spoken one, is probably who is responsible for removing Miss Spencer's arm. If she regained consciousness whilst he was carrying out this atrocious act, he may now have some nasty scratches on his face."

"How do you know all of this, old fellow?" asked Watson.

"Consider what we know, Watson. She was hit from behind and fell forwards, smashing her face into the kerb. We will probably find some of her missing teeth at the scene of this attack. Whilst laying face down on the kerb, she would not have been in a position to scratch anyone. She was, I suspect, loaded into a carriage and…" Holmes stopped, mid sentence.

He turned to Dr. Death, and asked, "May I see her clothing?"

Chapter 7

Dr. Death fetched a small sack, and emptied its contents onto an examination table. Holmes sifted through the garments. Her cloak showed a scuff mark, where she had fallen, and there were a lot of blood stains upon her upper garments. Every item of her clothing had blood stained hand prints all over it. Most revealing, however, was that her blouse still had its left sleeve intact and the stitching around the shoulder was undamaged.

Holmes continued from where he had left off. "When she had been dragged into the carriage, the smaller of the two men removed her clothing and started to saw her left arm off. At this point, the girl was not dead. The sudden pain she experienced, when he started sawing, caused her to regain consciousness. She struck her attacker with her right hand, and scratched his face. The print on her throat is from a shoe, or boot, and suggests that the man stamped on her, in reprisal for scratching him. It was probably at this time that, in his anger, he thrust his walking cane twice into her face. Judging by the size of the mark on her throat, left by the shoe, or boot, I would venture that the man is approximately 5 feet, 8 inches to 5 feet 10 inches tall."

"That's incredible, Holmes. But how do you know that it was the smaller, well spoken man that cut the girl's arm off?" enquired Lestrade.

"Firstly, the size of the print on the girl's throat is far too small to belong to the larger of the men. Secondly, I suspect the well spoken man to be Stephen Wood. If so, he will have hired the larger man as his muscle, but will be compelled to carry out as many of the gruesome acts as possible. I believe that he will derive a twisted pleasure in conducting such mutilations."

"You mentioned that the killer is likely to have been scratched on his face, by Sally Spencer. What leads to believe that the scratch will be on his face?" asked Watson.

"It was freezing cold last night, Watson. Anyone out in that weather would have been wrapped up in thick clothes. This leads me to think that the only parts of the killer's anatomy not covered by clothing, would have been his face and, possibly, his hands. Since he was using his hands to saw off the girl's arm, his face would have been in range of such an attack."

Holmes turned to Dr. Death, and asked, "May I examine the bodies to the two policemen?"

"Of course," replied the doctor.

Holmes began to examine the two dead policemen, whilst the other three men looked on.

After a short time, Holmes commented, "Both of these men appear to have been hit around the head with something like a shovel, moreover a clean shovel." He pointed out the marks on the dead bodies to the three onlookers, and then drew their attention to a small pin prick in the left arm of each policeman. "It also appears that the policemen were injected with something, which may have caused them to convulse, violently. Look at all the bruises, especially around their feet, ankles, elbows and wrists," he added.

Chapter 7

Dr. Death responded, "I also noticed those marks, Mr. Holmes. I can't be completely sure, at this stage, but I think they may have been injected with strychnine. If a lethal dose of strychnine is given, it causes convulsions. Death is usually caused by asphyxia or sheer exhaustion from the intensity of the convulsions. The bruises you mentioned are consistent with somebody experiencing a violent fit of some kind."

"I agree," said Holmes. "Let us move on to the trade marks of our killer. As you can see, P.C. Roach's right arm and Sergeant Baxter's right leg have been removed. Both appear to have been cut off with an axe, or similar instrument. The wounds show similarities, so I believe the same weapon was used in both cases. This mark appears on both wounds and was probably caused by a defect on the blade. Judging by the depth of the cuts, I would venture that Stephen Wood carried out this act, but it was the stronger accomplice that hit them with the shovel."

Nobody questioned the detective on what he had said, so he continued, "I believe that the girl was attacked between 11pm and 11:30pm last night, based upon the information her sister gave us. The policemen were probably killed some time after that."

"How do you know that?" questioned Watson.

"The clue is in the use of strychnine on the policemen, Watson. If I am correct about Miss Spencer attacking Stephen Wood after he thought her to be dead, it would have scared him. In order to avoid any further occurrences, he got his accomplice to attack the

The Dark Reckoning

policemen, on his behalf, with the shovel to make certain they would be rendered unconscious. After that, both were injected with strychnine to ensure that they were dead, before their limbs were removed. May I see their clothing please, Dr. Death?"

Dr. Death showed the clothing to Holmes. As with the clothing of the other victims, nothing was damaged except for the blood stains. Holmes examined the garments, but didn't discover anything of use.

He turned to Lestrade and asked, "May we return with you to Scotland Yard to find out where the bodies were found?"

"Of course you can, Holmes. Would you like to go there now?"

"Unless Dr. Death has any further information to share, then I should like to go now."

Dr. Death shook his head and said, "At this point, I can't tell you anymore than you already know. I may be in a position to give you more information later. Good day, gentlemen."

The three men bid the doctor farewell as they left, and returned to Scotland Yard. Just inside the entrance, a group of policemen were discussing their dead colleagues. They stopped talking when they saw Inspector Lestrade enter, with Holmes and Watson.

Chapter 7

The three men walked over to the group and Lestrade asked, "Were you just talking about the murders of Sergeant Baxter and P.C. Roach last night?"

"Yes, Sir," replied one of the officers. "It's terrible, Sir! Things like that just shouldn't happen. It could be one of us next!"

The inspector addressed the group. "Listen men. It is important that we continue to uphold the law. We *can't* let something like this distract us from our duty. It's a difficult time for all of us and we have to stick together. Can I count on you all?"

The men all nodded in agreement.

Holmes then addressed them. "May I ask where the policemen were found?"

"They were both in a field, Sir. Sardinia Fields, just by Lincoln's Inn," answered one of the officers.

"Yes, I know where that is. It's about 4 miles to the west of Holborn Viaduct," said Holmes.

"That's right," commented Lestrade. "The men hold a weekly card game near there, and I expect that Baxter and Roach would have been there last night."

"Does this card game take place *every* week?" asked Watson.

"It does, and it's normally the same group that play, except for those on duty."

The Dark Reckoning

"Whereabouts do these card games take place?" enquired Holmes.

"In Red Lion Street. It's about half a mile from where the bodies were found. I've been a couple of times in the past, but not for over a year. The games normally go on until past one in the morning. That's too late for me," replied Lestrade.

"Watson and I must leave now, Lestrade. We will try to establish what we can about the girl's death, and will be in touch later."

"Very well, Holmes. I'll go and speak to the Chief about Baxter and Roach. I will let him know about the connection between their deaths and those of Sir Charles Grey and Miss Spencer."

Holmes and Watson left Scotland Yard and walked under the archway, where Holmes suddenly stopped and looked at the pool of blood.

"The girl has been dragged from that direction," he said, pointing towards Whitehall.

He stepped under the barrier, followed by Watson, and walked through the crowd. When he got to a point where there were fewer people, he started walking much more slowly, whilst looking around on the ground.

After several minutes of this, he turned to Watson and said, "A carriage stopped just here, Watson." He pointed out the tracks, still visible in the morning frost, and continued, "The carriage had four wheels, indicated by

Chapter 7

these tracks. Furthermore, the distance between the left and right tracks shows it was a large carriage. Note the markings in the tracks themselves. We may find similar tracks at the scene where Miss Spencer was first attacked. The frost now covering the tracks leads me to believe that they were left some time ago; probably at about midnight, if Miss Spencer was at the theatre until around 11pm. The coach had been travelling south before it came to a stop."

"How can you tell that, Holmes?"

Holmes smiled and pointed at the tracks, as he explained, "See how the tracks show where the wheels locked as the carriage came to a halt. These small mounds of grit to the side of the skid marks reveal the direction the carriage must have been travelling."

"Oh yes, I see. But how can you be sure that this carriage was used to bring the body of the dead girl? Isn't it possible that Miss Spencer was attacked here?"

"According to her sister, Miss Spencer would have made her way directly from the theatre to her flat. Whitehall would have been too far out of her way. I believe she was attacked elsewhere, and then brought here in the carriage. As I suggested in the morgue, it is likely that her arm was removed whilst inside the carriage. Her attacker would have wanted to avoid being discovered, when conducting such a grizzly act."

"Yes, but I still can't see why you believe it was the carriage that left *these* tracks that brought the girl here."

The Dark Reckoning

"Imagine where the door of the carriage would be, if it stopped here. This blood on the ground corresponds exactly to where the carriage door would have been." replied Holmes pointing out several blood spots on the pavement. "That's why I believe these are the tracks of the carriage that brought the dead girl here."

Holmes took a piece of paper and pencil from his pocket and started to draw the pattern left by each of the four tracks. He then took a handkerchief and wiped some of the blood from the pavement onto it. He placed the handkerchief into a small bag and then asked, "What time is it, Watson?"

"Five minutes before ten, old fellow."

"Good! Come along, Watson! Let us find where Miss Spencer was attacked."

The two men walked to Trafalgar Square, and into a small butcher's shop on the corner of Cockspur Street.

The owner looked pleased to see the two gentlemen, with a broad smile, said, "Good mornin' to you, Mr. Holmes, and to you, Dr. Watson. What can I do for you?"

"We should like to use the services of Ginny for a while, Mr. Bloomfield," replied Holmes.

"I see," said the butcher, suddenly looking far more serious. "What's happened? Are you workin' on a case?"

Chapter 7

"Yes, we are," answered Holmes. "There isn't a great deal that I can tell you at present, but I do believe Ginny may be able to help".

"Fair enough, Mr. Holmes. Wait here a minute." The butcher went through a door at the back of the shop, and called up to his wife. He returned to the shop, followed, a few moments later, by his wife.

"Darling', Mr. Holmes wants to borrow Ginny. Can you look after the shop for a few minutes?" asked the butcher.

"Of course," smiled Mrs. Bloomfield, warmly. "How are you gentlemen today?" she asked Holmes and Watson.

"Very well, thank you, Mrs. Bloomfield," replied Watson. "How are you?"

"I'm well, thank you."

"Come through, gentlemen," said the butcher, leading the way into the living quarters at the back of the shop.

He led them into the living room, where Ginny, a smooth haired fox terrier, was curled in front of a large fire. She looked up as the three men entered the room. Her tail immediately started wagging, excitedly, as she got up to greet them. Holmes squatted and made a fuss of the small dog, and attached a lead that Mr. Bloomfield handed to him.

Holmes and Watson left the shop with Ginny, via the back garden, and made their way to Scotland Yard. They allowed Ginny to sniff around the blood where the body of Miss Spencer had been dumped and, also, where the carriage had stopped. After this, they made their way to The Theatre Royal, Haymarket and discussed the likely routes that Sally Spencer may have taken from the theatre the previous night.

"Sally Spencer was making her way to Charing Cross Road, wasn't she, Holmes?" asked Watson.

"Yes. She could have continued along Haymarket to Coventry Street and turned right. However, I think she would have favoured the quieter roads as it would have been quicker. Let us try Orange Street as a starting point."

As the two men turned into Orange Street, Holmes took the handkerchief he had wiped the blood found at Scotland Yard onto, and let Ginny sniff it. Ginny led them along Orange Street, but seemed unsure which way to proceed when they reached the junction of Whitcomb Street. Holmes let her sniff the handkerchief again, but she didn't pick up any scent.

"It would make sense if Miss Spencer travelled in a northerly direction from here, Holmes," ventured Watson.

"I agree, Watson. Let us cross the road and walk along Whitcomb Street. Perhaps Ginny will pick the scent up from there."

At 11:30am, Ginny led the men into Lisle Street and began to pull on her lead. She took them directly to a blood stain on the kerb. Holmes squatted down to examine the immediate area. He discovered two teeth in

Chapter 7

the gutter and a few strands of blonde hair, stuck to a small piece of blood soaked skin on the edge of the kerb. Blood was splattered across the pavement and a thick line of it was smeared off of the edge of the kerb into the road. There were tracks from a carriage visible in the frost that matched the tracks found at Scotland Yard. Furthermore, there were two sets of footprints visible, one of which matched the mark found on the dead girl's throat. The other set of footprints were considerably larger.

"Well, Watson," said Holmes. "This is where the initial assault appears to have taken place. Thanks to Ginny's acute sense of smell, we have found the scene of Miss Spencer's attack. These would appear to be her footprints, which suggest that she was walking towards her sister's home and was stalked from behind. And look!" Holmes pointed to a nearby gate.

"What is it?" asked Watson following Holmes' gaze.

"Over there! It's a hammer!" Holmes ran over to the hammer and stooped down to look at it more closely.

Watson followed, asking, "Is that the weapon used on Miss Spencer, Holmes?"

"It appears so, Watson. As you can see, it is covered with blood. If you look more closely, there are strands of hair stuck on the head of the hammer that match Miss Spencer's in colour and length."

Both Watson and Holmes made sketches and notes of all they could see at the crime scene and then placed the items they had discovered into bags.

The Dark Reckoning

Holmes turned to Watson, and said, "We shall take these items to Scotland Yard soon, Watson. Before doing so, let us see if we can retrace the attacker's footsteps."

With the help of Ginny, they were able to trace back to where the man had hidden himself behind a garden wall in Leicester Street the previous night. Watson noticed a cigarette that had been stamped out when only about half finished. "Look here, Holmes. Somebody put a cigarette out, before finishing it."

"Well spotted, Watson. The boot print surrounding the cigarette does appear to match the larger of the footprints we found in Lisle Street. I expect he was waiting here for Miss Spencer, and decided to smoke. Upon hearing her approach, he put the cigarette out and hid behind this wall. His footprints are easily discernable in this flower bed."

"That makes perfect sense, Holmes. Can you deduce anything else?"

"Judging by the prints left by his shoes, or boots, I would imagine that the attacker is a fairly poor man. The tread is very well worn, as shown by the indentations in the flower bed. Furthermore, the right footprint shows more wear than the left, so it is possible that the attacker may suffer a slight limp affecting his right leg."

"If he spent time waiting here, somebody may have noticed him," commented Watson.

"Bravo, Watson! That is entirely plausible." Holmes looked at the surrounding houses and noticed a middle aged woman staring at him through a window.

Chapter 7

"Ah, she appears to be somewhat inquisitive," he mentioned, "Let us go and speak to her."

Holmes collected the stamped out cigarette and made his way to the front door, with Watson. He was about to knock on the door when it was pulled open from within by the woman who had just been looking from the window.

She stared coldly at the two men and snapped, "What do ya' want, snooping around 'ere?"

"My name is Sherlock Holmes, and I am investigating a crime that took place in this area last night. Did you see anything, or anyone, suspicious last night?"

The woman's eyes narrowed as she looked at Holmes. After a short pause, she asked, "What sort of crime?"

"A young lady was murdered," answered Watson.

"Oh, no. What is this world comin' to?" asked the woman rhetorically. Her stare softened and she continued, "I saw a bloke hangin' around outside. It was just after eleven last night when I saw 'im. He was pacin' around for about ten or fifteen minutes. All of a sudden, he hid in the garden where I just saw you two."

"Can you describe this man?" asked Holmes.

"All I can really say is that he was big. It was a foggy night, so I didn't get much of a look."

"Is there anything else you remember about him?"

The Dark Reckoning

"Come to think of it, I saw him smoking a cigarette. When he lit it and the match was near 'is face, I think I saw a scar on 'is right cheek. Can't be completely sure though."

"What happened after he had hidden himself behind the garden wall?" asked Watson.

"He waited there for about five minutes and then suddenly came out of the garden and walked into Lisle Street, deary," replied the woman smiling, showing off her rotten brown teeth.

"Please continue," prompted Holmes.

"I didn't like the look of the bloke. At first, I was too scared to follow, but after a bit, I wanted to make sure that 'e was gone. I went into Lisle Street and there was a big carriage. The bloke I 'ad seen was there wiv' another one. They lifted someone into the carriage, and then the bigger bloke climbed up into the driver's seat. The other bloke looked around and then got inside. After that the carriage started to move towards me, so I hid until it was gone."

"Can you describe the shorter of the two men?" asked Holmes.

"I suppose 'e might have been about the same height as your friend," she answered, pointing at Watson. She then went on, "I only got a glimpse. He was a bit ugly. He had fat, round lips. I can't tell you anyfing else. I only saw that much 'cos 'e stood near a streetlight for a moment."

Chapter 7

Holmes smiled at the woman and said, "Thank you. You have been extremely helpful."

"Anytime, deary. I hope you catch 'em," said the woman, as she closed the door and went inside.

As the two men turned away, Holmes said, "I think we had better return Ginny to Mr. Bloomfield."

The men walked the dog along Whitcomb Street, towards Trafalgar Square.

On their way, Holmes asked, "When the woman described the shorter of the two men, who did it remind you of, Watson?"

"Erm… Her description matches what we know of our suspect, so I would say that it is Stephen Wood."

"Anyone else?" prompted Holmes

"No, I don't think so, Holmes."

"Imagine if he wore a beard and moustache. Can you picture anyone apart from the suspect?"

"No, I'm afraid that I can't, Holmes. Who do you have in mind?"

Holmes paused, perhaps for dramatic effect, and then replied, "Arthur Smith."

The Dark Reckoning

"But it can't be! When I left Paignton, he was so busy working on his farm and said that he would not be coming to London for several months."

"Could the description, the lady just gave us, apply to Arthur Smith, Watson?" asked Holmes with persistence in his voice.

Watson thought for a moment before replying, in an unconvinced manner, "Well, I suppose it could, Holmes. But her description could apply to any of several men! I don't understand why you are trying to establish a connection between the description and Arthur."

"I am not entirely convinced that the primary purpose of your visit to Arthur's farm was to help him get settled in."

A look of shock developed on Watson's face, as he snapped, "That is preposterous! All I did the entire time I was with Arthur was to help out on the farm. You are being ridiculous!" His voice became more raised as he spoke and his eyes narrowed, indicating his growing anger.

"I have no doubt that you spent the majority of your time helping Arthur, but I still believe there was another reason for your visit," added Holmes, as he watched Watson's lips stiffen and his face flush.

Watson stopped walking and, glaring at Holmes, shouted, "How *dare* you accuse me of being a liar, Sir! I *demand* you explain yourself!" Watson's fists were bunched, as he continued glaring at Holmes, awaiting a response.

Chapter 7

"Calm yourself, Watson. I am accusing you of no such thing."

"Yes you are!" came the angered response.

Holmes smiled briefly, amused at how easily Watson became annoyed.

"Would you please allow me to elucidate?" he asked in a voice somewhat too calm.

Watson looked around, not sure quite what to do. He knew that Holmes would have an explanation that would render his anger pointless. Despite still feeing irritated at Holmes, he was also curious.

After a few moments he said, somewhat sarcastically, "Very well. Please *do* elucidate."

"Tell me, Watson, did you get drunk at any point during your time with Arthur?"

All remaining anger immediately drained out of Watson, as Holmes' question sparked a memory from his visit to Devon.

"You are incredible, Holmes. How did you know? One evening, Arthur suggested that we share some wine. After only half a glass, or so, I remember feeling very strange. I looked at my glass and realised that I shouldn't be feeling so drunk. I don't remember anything else from that point until the next morning."

The Dark Reckoning

"How did you feel the next morning? Were you suffering with a hangover?"

"That's another odd thing. I felt slightly groggy, but it wasn't as bad as a hangover."

"I believe you were drugged, Watson."

"Surely not, Holmes. Smith is such a decent fellow. What possible reason could he have to drug me?"

"I fear that he wanted to gain information from you, old fellow. It is my firm belief that Arthur Smith and Stephen Wood are the same man. If I am correct, he tricked you into visiting him, with the intention of getting you to reveal information about people connected to the trial of his brother."

"Are you serious? Do you really believe that Arthur Smith is actually Stephen Wood? What information would I have been in a position to give him?"

"Stephen Wood was never present at his brother's trial. From what I recall, he had been committed to the lunatic asylum before his brother's case came to court. Therefore, he was not privy to any details of the witnesses, or other people involved in securing Stanley Wood's conviction."

Holmes paused, as he felt awkward about what he needed to say next. He then continued, "Watson, it is my belief that you, unwittingly, provided Stephen Wood with details about his intended victims. He subsequently used

Chapter 7

this information to find and kill anyone he felt was responsible for the death of his brother."

Watson's face sank. He stood looking down at the ground and quietly said, "But that means people are being killed because of me."

Holmes placed a hand on Watson's shoulder and replied, reassuringly, "That isn't true, Watson. You are in no way responsible. You were tricked. The reason people are being killed is because someone, possibly Stephen Wood, is murdering them, not because of anything that you have done. Please try not to feel so bad, old fellow."

Watson looked up to see Holmes smiling at him. He still felt awful, as he asked, "How could I have been so easily fooled, Holmes? I never suspected *anything* about Arthur."

"Arthur Smith, or should I say Stephen Wood, fooled us both, Watson. With his beard and glasses, it would have been difficult to have recognised him as Wood. I had noticed that he wore dark glasses, even when inside. Although I thought that strange, I accepted his explanation that he suffered from photophobia. Now, it seems more likely that he wore those glasses to hide his eyes from us."

Watson gave a dejected sigh, but said nothing.

Holmes, concerned at how upset his friend was, added, "Watson, this is only a theory. I may not be correct about you being used in such an awful way. I may even be

The Dark Reckoning

wrong about Stephen Wood and Arthur Smith being the same man."

"I know you are trying to help, old man, but you are *always* right about these types of things."

"Not always, Watson." The reply seemed thoughtful, as though Holmes was looking inwards as he uttered the words. Watson noticed a hint of melancholy show on Holmes' face.

Holmes quickly snapped out of his thoughtfulness, and, with a smile, added, "Come along, Watson. We should take Ginny back home, and then deliver the items we found to Scotland Yard. After that, I have something that I would like to try out."

"What about Miss Spencer, Holmes?" asked Watson. "Should we not tell her about her sister?"

"Yes, of course. You are quite right, Watson. After we have taken Ginny home and delivered this evidence to Scotland Yard, we can take a Hansom cab to Charing Cross Road."

After taking Ginny back to Mr. Bloomfield, the two men found a Hansom cab to take them to Scotland Yard, where the handed all the evidence they had gathered to Inspector Lestrade, and gave him a description of the crime scene. Following this, they continued their journey to see Miss Spencer. Neither of the men spoke during the journey.

They arrived at 28 Charing Cross Road and knocked on the door, which was opened, shortly after, by Susan

Chapter 7

Spencer. She looked anxious upon seeing the two men, and felt an odd mixture of dread and hope. She hoped that her ambivalence would soon be over, as she asked, "Mr. Holmes! Have you any news of my sister?"

Holmes replied, ignoring the question, "May we come in, Miss Spencer?"

"Yes, of course. Please come in. We shall adjourn to my room."

Holmes noticed that Susan Spencer was trembling, as she led them up a flight of stairs and into a pleasantly decorated room. He removed his hat and coat and Watson followed suit.

"May I sit down, Miss Spencer?" asked Holmes, hoping that his question would also prompt the girl to sit.

"Yes, please do," she replied, pointing to a sofa. She came and sat next to Holmes and looked at him expectantly, but found that she was too afraid to ask anything.

Holmes looked at Susan, and quietly said, "I have news of your sister, Miss Spencer. I'm afraid... I..." He stared down at the floor, unable to finish the sentence or look her in the eye.

"*Please* tell me, Mr. Holmes," implored Miss Spencer, shakily.

Holmes looked back up at the distraught girl as she grabbed his forearm.

The Dark Reckoning

She looked deeply into the detective's eyes and added, "I fear I already know what you are going to say, Mr. Holmes, but I need to… I have to…" Her voice became chocked with emotion. She looked through the blur of her tears at Mr. Holmes, and could see that he was trying so hard to find the right words to say.

Suddenly, she felt a sadness so deep as, for the first time, she realised that she would never see Sally again. Her mind flooded with so many fond memories of her sister, which contrasted so greatly with the emptiness she envisioned for her future. She could not conceive a life without Sally and wanted a chance to be able to make more fond memories. More than anything, she wanted to see her again. Instead, all she could imagine for her future was an unfulfilled void of despair.

She sobbed her saddest tears, whilst still holding onto Holmes' forearm. She would have given anything to be able to see Sally again.

A thought flashed through Susan's mind. Perhaps Sally *was* alive. Mr. Holmes had not told her anything yet. Perhaps Sally had been badly hurt, but would recover. A faint glimmer of hope showed in her eyes as she looked up at Holmes.

She forced her voice past her unwilling lips, and managed to whisper, "Please, tell me, Mr. Holmes."

Without realising, Holmes gently placed his hand on top of Susan's. His voice was soft, as he said, "I am so sorry, Miss Spencer. Your sister is dead."

Chapter 7

Her crying became more insistent and her weeping voice whispered, "Oh, God... No... No."

She saw the image of Sally's face in her mind's eye, the vision, so vivid, was merely an illusion created by her broken heart. The image changed to that of a dead body, lying motionless on a table in a morgue. The vision of her dead sister, with open lifeless eyes and pale blue skin, haunted Susan's mind.

As she began to acquaint herself with the loneliness of life without her sister, her weakened voice asked, "Why is she dead?"

Holmes looked into Susan's saddened eyes and quietly answered, "There is no good reason. An act of murder is a violation that cruelly robs the world of someone special. Even though she has gone, she will live on in your memories. Nobody can take those from you."

A fresh stream of tears ran down Susan's face, but, at the same time, she smiled.

"Thank you, Mr. Holmes. You are right. She meant so much to me. She was always so strong, and was always there when I needed her. Although I won't be able to turn to her from now, I will always remember her. But now that she has gone, who will I be able to turn to?"

Holmes sat silently, unable to find words to console the weeping girl at his side.

After a short pause, Susan continued, "I always took her for granted. I just expected that she would always be a part of my life. I never told her that I loved her, and now I will never be able to. She died not knowing how much I loved her."

Watson came over with a glass of water he had poured for Susan.

"She knew how much you loved her, Miss Spencer; in the same way that you always knew how much she loved you," said Watson, as he handed her the water.

"Thank you, Dr. Watson," acknowledged Susan. She took a sip and became aware of how much her hands were trembling as she held the glass. Holmes also noticed, so he took the glass from her and set it on a nearby table.

She smiled at him and asked, "Why is it that I am able to tell you, a perfect stranger, how much I cared for Sally, but I was never able to tell her? I could never say the words 'I love you' to her."

"It is just the way people are, Miss Spencer," responded Holmes. "We spend a great deal of time concealing our emotions, in part to protect ourselves because they make us vulnerable. I also believe that society has conditioned us to hide our emotions to such an extent, that we are now afraid to ever reveal them. Perhaps, because we cannot control our emotions, we have become too afraid to share them."

Susan sat, feeling the warmth of Holmes' hand on hers, as she quietly cried and shook her head. She sat in silence for a minute, or so, her bloodshot eyes staring at the crackling fireplace.

Chapter 7

Her gaze moved to Holmes as she said, "Sally had some good news to tell me last night. I already knew, but was still looking forward to hearing her tell me. She was going to be married. I had even been practicing how to act surprised when she told me." A faint smile appeared on Susan's face as she continued, "I remember when we were children. Sally never wanted to get married. She used to say that boys were horrid. Life was so simple back then."

Susan's brief smile turned, once again, to an expression of despair.

Her gaze returned to the fireplace and she added, "I don't know how I'll manage without Sally. I always depended on her and needed her in my life. Why did this have to happen, Mr. Holmes?"

She looked at Holmes and noticed an anguished expression on his face. She could see that he was averting his eyes, avoiding her gaze. As she continued to look, waiting for him to answer, she saw a tear run down his cheek. He opened his mouth slightly, as if to speak, but no words came.

After a pause, he looked at Susan and said, in a voice barely above a whisper, "I am so sorry."

"It wasn't your fault, Mr. Holmes," replied Susan, sensing that Holmes felt, somehow, responsible.

Holmes smiled at her and, wiping his eyes, asked, "Is there anything that Dr. Watson and I can do for you, Miss Spencer?"

The Dark Reckoning

"No, thank you. I think I would like to be left alone. You... You are going to catch her... her killer, aren't you?"

Holmes looked at the girl and thought, 'it will be a long time before your sadness passes.'

He stood up to leave and replied, "You can be assured that Dr. Watson and I will make every endeavour to catch this murderer, Miss Spencer. If you need us for anything, anything at all, please contact us. We will leave you now."

"Thank you, Mr. Holmes and you too, Dr. Watson."

As the two men walked out of the front door, Holmes turned to the girl and said, "You will receive a visit from the police soon, confirming what I have already told you, Miss Spencer. They will probably require you to provide them with a positive identification of your sister. If you would like me and Dr. Watson to accompany you, we will be available. Goodbye, Miss Spencer. I hope your grieving turns to fond memories soon."

Out in the street, Watson turned to Holmes and asked, "Are you alright, Holmes?"

"Yes, old fellow. Let us return home as there is something that I should like to try, after lunch."

Chapter 8

Chapter 8

"Absolutely, out of the question!"

"Please try to understand, Watson. This is our best chance."

"Be that as it may, Holmes, there is *no* way I can condone such foolishness."

"I only wish to hypnotise you, Watson. This is something that I have studied, and I believe that it may help us catch Stephen Wood, if he is our killer."

The Dark Reckoning

"This is preposterous. You can't possibly believe that hypnotising me will help to catch the killer," retorted Watson, angrily.

"As I have already stated, Watson, I suspect Arthur Smith to be none other than Stephen Wood."

"Do you really think that it was Stephen Wood masquerading as Arthur?" asked Watson, in a considerably less angry voice.

"Yes, I do, Watson. If I can get you into a relaxed and receptive state, you may tell me some of the details that I believe you revealed when he drugged you."

"I must confess that, when you suggested Arthur Smith was, in fact, Stephen Wood, I was more shocked than convinced, Holmes. I still don't feel sure that Arthur could be Stephen Wood."

Holmes walked over to the table, moved the lunch plates out of the way and grabbed a stack of files that he started to sort through. When he had found what he was looking for, he took it to Watson.

He held out a photograph for Watson and said, "This is a photograph of Stephen Wood, taken just before he was committed. Can you see the resemblance now?"

Watson shook his head and replied, hesitantly, "I do see the resemblance, but I can't be sure."

Holmes smiled, expecting Watson's reply. He took a piece of tracing paper and placed it over the photograph

Chapter 8

and drew a beard and moustache, as well as some darkened glasses. He then showed the composite image to Watson.

"My God, Holmes! You *are* right. That looks *exactly* like Arthur Smith."

"Another indication is that Stephen Wood was released from the asylum approximately six months ago, at about the same time we first made the acquaintance of Arthur Smith. In addition, we discovered that the meat cleaver used to kill Sir Charles Grey was purchased at a shop called Smiths. This may simply be a coincidence, but perhaps not."

"Oh, I think that must be a coincidence, Holmes."

"Possibly, Watson, but it could also be the reason that Stephen Wood chose 'Smith' as a pseudonym. I believe that he sees himself as extremely clever. He may have decided to provide subtle and intelligent clues about his identity, that he thought nobody would ever determine."

Watson sat quietly for a moment, stroking his chin, as he considered what Holmes was proposing to him.

He then looked up and asked, "If I agree to your idea of hypnotising me, would I be in any danger? After all, you are not a trained hypnotist."

Holmes laughed as he replied, "Of course there is no danger, old fellow. Hypnosis is not so powerful as to allow me to control, or alter, your mind. All I can do is help you relax into a peaceful and receptive state. Whilst in this state, your unconscious mind may be able to reveal details that your conscious mind has forgotten. My attempt may not have any effect at all, but I can guarantee that I can't possibly do you any harm."

"Do you *really* know what you are doing, Holmes?"

"Yes, I do, Watson. Perhaps, what I am about to say will convince you. As you may recall, Stanley Wood used to keep a body part from each of his victims. He went on to join these body parts together, by sewing them. He ended up constructing a complete composite body, made up of all the parts he had collected. Our new murderer has already severed a head, two arms and a right leg. He now requires a left leg and a torso to make a complete body, so I believe that he plans to commit at least two more murders."

"Who do you think his next intended victims might be?"

"Since it was you and I that caught Stanley Wood, I believe that we are the next intended victims."

Watson looked visibly shaken, as he answered, "Very well, Holmes, you can hypnotise me. If I can reveal any clue that might help catch this lunatic, it will be worth it."

Under hypnosis, Watson revealed that Stephen Wood had asked a lot of questions about Holmes. Watson also confirmed that he had told Wood the names of the witnesses and the judge at his brother's trial. He then mentioned the address '15 Lower Thames Street', which he felt had some significance, although he could not recall

Chapter 8

why. When Holmes had finished the hypnosis, he snapped his fingers and Watson awoke.

"Come along, old fellow," said Holmes, with a hint of excitement in his voice.

"Where are we going?"

"We are going to 15 Lower Thames Street. You mentioned this address whilst under hypnosis, but could not recall its significance."

The two men left Baker Street and took a cab to London Bridge. Having alighted, Holmes asked the cab driver to wait. Holmes noticed a small road, called Arthur Street, which was situated on the opposite side of the road from where he was standing. He wondered whether this could have any connection with the reason that Stephen Wood had chosen the name, Arthur.

Holmes and Watson walked along Lower Thames Street until they found number 15. It was a somewhat run down looking place. Although the buildings could not be considered slums, they all seemed quite grimy. Number 15 was no exception and looked dingy. Its windows were dirty and had old looking net curtains hanging inside, making it impossible to see what was within.

Holmes turned to Watson and said, "I shall wait here, whilst you take the cab to Scotland Yard and fetch Lestrade. Tell him that I should like him to bring a few officers with him." Holmes looked around the area and then continued, "That small alley over the road shall afford me suitable cover and provide a good vantage point to observe number 15. I shall be there when you return."

"Why do you wish to remain here, Holmes?"

"It is possible that this is the address Stephen Wood is using, whilst in London. I intend to observe whether there is any activity inside whilst waiting for you to return, with Lestrade and his men."

"What leads you to believe that this may be where Wood is based?"

"It first struck me when you mentioned it, whilst under hypnosis. You seemed convinced that there was a connection, but were unable to say what it could be. It is possible that Wood revealed the address to you, without telling you anything about it. Furthermore, the name of a road near to where we left the cab is Arthur Street. Perhaps that is why Wood chose the pseudonym, 'Arthur'."

Watson stood thinking for a while, before responding, "Holmes, I don't like the idea of you waiting here alone. If Wood and his accomplice are using number 15, you could be in danger."

"Thank you for your concern, Watson. I will place myself out of site, in the alley. I promise not to take any action until you return," replied Holmes, with a smile on his face.

Watson left and made his way back to the waiting cab, whilst Holmes walked over to the alley and found a

Chapter 8

suitable spot, from where he could observe number 15. He glanced at his pocket watch to check the time, which was 4:05pm. Holmes thought, 'It will soon be dark,' as he noticed the light was already beginning to fade.

As he waited, the light became dimmer and mist started creeping up from the river. The coldness numbed Holmes' feet, as he stood watching number 15. He saw no movement from within and nobody entered, or left, the building.

At 4:35pm, Holmes glanced at his watch again and had just placed it back in his pocket, when he heard footsteps behind him. As he turned to see who was approaching, two hands suddenly grabbed his arms. Holmes stared at the man who had grabbed him. Although it was starting to get dark, Holmes could see his adversary's face was pitted and had a small scar on the right cheek. The man was much bigger, and stronger, than Holmes and easily pushed him out of the alley and into the street. Holmes turned to fight, but the man produced a knife. The knife was quickly placed against Holmes' throat. The man stepped behind Holmes, still holding the knife against his throat. Holmes winced, as the larger man grabbed his left arm and forced it up against his back. The man then pushed Holmes over Lower Thames Street to the doorway of number 15.

The larger man forced Holmes' arm higher behind his back, as he withdrew the knife and unlocked the door. Once inside, Holmes was forced up a flight of stairs and into a room on the first floor.

Inside the room, a man sat facing the door. Upon seeing Holmes, a hideously smug smile broke out on his face.

"Mr. Holmes!" he exclaimed, in a strangely triumphant sounding voice.

"Stephen Wood! I *knew* I would find you here."

"And, I knew you would come here. You have fallen into my trap, just as I knew you would."

Holmes ignored the comment and asked, "Tell me, how is that scratch on the side of your face? I see that Miss Spencer managed to draw blood."

The smile vanished from Wood's face, as he retorted, "How do you know that *bitch* did this to me?" He pointed to the scratch on his face, whilst staring, coldly, at Holmes.

"I know a great deal about you, Wood. I know that, upon being released from the asylum, you put into action a plan you had conceived to avenge your brother's execution. You set about murdering those you saw as responsible for Stanley's conviction. You even chose to use his trade mark of removing body parts. May I enquire as to why you befriended me and Dr. Watson, under the pseudonym, Arthur Smith?"

"In part, it was to find out more about those responsible for my brother's murder."

Chapter 8

Holmes shook his head upon hearing the misuse of the word 'murder' to describe a legal execution, but he chose to say nothing.

Wood smirked, as he continued, "My primary reason, however, was to find out more about you, Mr. Holmes."

"To what end?"

"I needed to establish how I could arouse your interest, when I started to kill those people. After having known you for a while, I..."

"And after having drugged Watson," interrupted Holmes. The comment caused a brief look of worry to appear on Wood's face, which led Holmes to believe the murderer had underestimated him.

The worried expression was fleeting, as Wood continued, "Yes, I did drug Watson, and gained a lot of useful information. Anyhow, I decided that, by not damaging the clothing of my victims, you would soon become interested in pursuing the case. To ensure that you began to realise these killings were in revenge for the death of Stanley, I chose to adopt his trade mark of retaining a body part from each of my victims. I have even started to sew the pieces together, as it seemed such a fitting epitaph to my poor dead brother."

Holmes felt exultant at having his suspicions proved correct, although he knew it would be foolish to underestimate Wood. He felt sure that Wood had also anticipated a lot of the steps that he had taken to discover the truth.

The Dark Reckoning

Holmes' happiness was short lived, as Wood went on, "I'm sure you realize that I am going to kill both you and Dr. Watson. Then, I will have disposed of all six people responsible for my brother's death. I intend to remove your head and limbs, so that I may use your trunk as part of my composite body. That will leave a left leg, which will be supplied by Dr. Watson."

Wood got up from his chair and walked across the room, to a blood stained curtain that lay on the floor. He lifted it to unveil the body parts that he had sewn together.

Holmes turned his head away in disgust and said, "You will not get away with these crimes. The police are already on their way."

"Shut up, you fool!" snapped the killer, "Nothing you can say will stop me killing you. I don't *care* if the police catch me! I know that I am destined to be hanged for the people I have killed. I always knew it would be the price I would have to pay in order to avenge my poor brother." The words were spoken with such venom that Holmes had no doubt that Wood really didn't care about his own life. It was as though he was entirely consumed by a hateful need for, what he saw as, retribution.

Wood slowly paced around the room, all the while staring at Holmes. He said nothing, as he continued to pace. Holmes became more anxious as every minute passed, and wondered where Watson and the police were.

He tried to free himself from the large man, who now gripped both of his arms, but could not do so. The man was simply too strong.

Chapter 8

Eventually, Wood stopped pacing. As he stared at Holmes, a twisted smile formed on his face. His eyes slowly looked towards his accomplice.

Holmes felt a sudden terror, as he heard Wood say, "You can kill him now, Jack."

The Dark Reckoning

Chapter 9

Holmes crashed into a wall near the room's entrance, as he was shoved, with immense ferocity, by the larger of the two men.

Having heard Wood mention the name, Jack, Holmes now knew who this man was. His name was Jack Roberts. He had been a fairly well known wrestler, until he seriously hurt an opponent in a fight that ended his career.

Jack grabbed Holmes by the collars and thrust him back into the wall once again. The force drove the breath from Holmes' body and he was temporarily stunned. Before he could recompose himself, Jack repeated the movement causing the back of Holmes' head to hit the wall. Holmes

Chapter 9

collapsed to the ground, completely dazed, as Jack released his grip.

In his semi-conscious state, Holmes observed the large man walk over to the other side of the room and pick up a shovel. Holmes desperately tried to pick himself up, but could not move. As the large man approached, Holmes became paralysed with terror. He felt his breath coming in short erratic bursts and his heart beating furiously.

Jack stood over Holmes, his eyes glaring madly and his teeth bared in an aggressive snarl. He raised the shovel above his head. Holmes saw the blur of the shovel as it hurtled down towards him, causing him to flinch sideways, but not far enough to avoid being hit. The shovel smashed into his left shoulder. A deadening pain rushed down his left arm, causing him to yell out loudly.

Once again, Jack raised the shovel above his head. This time, however, Holmes was able to move, having regained control of his senses. He raised his right leg and thrust his foot into Jack's left kneecap. The force of the kick caused the large man to shriek, as he fell backwards, dropping the shovel as he did so. Holmes saw his opportunity and immediately jumped to his feet. He grabbed the shovel and rushed towards Jack, with the intention of knocking him out.

As he approached Jack, he saw Wood pick up a bottle and throw it at him. The bottle struck him on the left shoulder, already injured by the blow from the shovel. This caused Holmes to stop and wince in pain. As he recomposed himself, Wood threw another bottle, which hit him on the back of the head and made him fall

The Dark Reckoning

forwards to the floor. As he was falling, Holmes realised how close he was to Jack. He bunched his right fist and managed to punch Jack on the side of his jaw. Holmes was beginning to think that he might be able to win this fight and started to stand, when Jack suddenly punched him in the stomach.

Holmes immediately collapsed on the floor, clutching at his stomach as his lungs fought to take in air. Jack stood and shoved Holmes with his foot, so that he rolled onto his back. The large man then sat astride Holmes' stomach and grabbed him by the collar with his left hand. He threw a punch with his right hand, aimed at Holmes' face. Somehow, Holmes jerked his head to the right, so that the punch skimmed his left ear and crashed into the wooden floor boards.

The unexpected pain sent Jack into such a furious rage, that he started to growl and wrapped both hands around Holmes' throat. He began to squeeze, choking Holmes, who tried to think of a way to stop this madman. He instinctively grabbed at Jack's wrists, and tried to pull them away from his throat, but to no avail. He then realised that he could easily reach Jack's chin, so he moved his hands in front of his own chin and then punched upwards with both hands at once.

The grip around his throat was instantly released, as his fists hit Jack's chin, and he gasped in air. Wood came to Jack's assistance and grabbed both of Holmes' hands so that the larger man could continue to strangle him. The large man smirked triumphantly, as he gripped Holmes' throat once more. As he started to squeeze, Holmes, unable to breath, began to panic. His heart started to

Chapter 9

pound in his chest and his lungs seemed to be frantically screaming for air. He desperately tried to free his arms from Wood's grip, but could not do so. As he struggled, he could feel his arms becoming weaker. His head started to pound with the agonising beat of his straining heart.

Holmes tried to shout, 'help me!' but all that emerged was a pitiful gurgle. He looked up at Jack, but all he could see was a blur. All the pain he felt started to fade away and he was aware that his heart beat was beginning to fail. He lost his ability to concentrate and began to feel a wonderful calmness. Somewhere in the distance, he thought he heard a loud bang and the pressure around his throat disappeared.

Holmes slowly opened his eyes and mumbled, "I thought I was dead." He heard a voice reply, but could not understand any of the words being spoken. His vision was blurred and took some time before it started to clear. As it did so, he felt a great relief, as he saw his friend, Dr. Watson looking over him.

"Watson," coughed Holmes, "What happened? Where is Jack?"

"Jack? Oh, you must mean the man who was strangling you. He is dead. I shot him in the back of the head. How are you, Holmes?" Watson's voice revealed his deep concern for Holmes.

The Dark Reckoning

"I think I am alright, thank you, Watson. Help me up, please, old chap," said Holmes, as he sat up.

"Of course. Are you certain that you are ready to stand?"

"Yes, I am certain," replied Holmes, smiling.

Watson helped Holmes to his feet. When he was standing, Holmes looked down at the crumpled body of Jack Roberts. Although he was dead, his eyes were still open and his mouth still bore a menacing grimace. Blood flowed from a large hole in his forehead, forming a growing pool on the floor.

"Where is Wood?" asked Holmes, with a sense of great urgency.

"As we entered the room, he ran and climbed out of the window onto the fire escape," answered Watson. "Lestrade and two of his men gave chase. I think he might have decided to go onto the roof, as Lestrade had deployed four officers in the street."

For the first time, Holmes observed that two policemen were also in the room. Not paying them any heed, he rushed across the room to the window, his desire for pursuit helping him forget the pain he was suffering.

"Come along, Watson," he called, as he climbed through the window. Watson followed suit and, together, they ascended the steps of the fire escape.

Below in the street, a small crowd had gathered, eagerly looking up at the roof. Lestrade and two officers were

Chapter 9

standing at the top of the fire escape. Holmes approached the top of the four-storey building, noticing the frost that had settled on the iron staircase, making it slippery.

As he joined the police officers at the top of the fire escape, he heard a voice shout, "Stay where you are!" He looked in the direction of the voice and saw Wood balancing precariously on the top of the roof, holding onto a chimney.

Watson joined the others at the top of the fire escape. Upon seeing Wood, he quietly said, "My God, Holmes. Do you think he will jump?"

Holmes did not acknowledge the question, but instead asked Lestrade, "Have you tried to get him to come down from there, Inspector?"

"Yes we have, Holmes. He won't come down. He said that he wants to speak to you and won't move until he has done so."

"Very well, let us play his game," replied Holmes. He moved himself in front of the police officers and called out, "Wood, this is Sherlock Holmes. What is it that you wish to tell me?"

The murderer looked over at Holmes and, in a mocking voice, called, "I intend to give you a chance to satisfy your insatiable need to catch criminals, Mr. Holmes."

Holmes felt the scorn in Wood's words, as he asked, "What do you mean, Wood?"

The Dark Reckoning

"You now know that I am the murderer you have been seeking, Mr. Holmes. Well, come and catch me."

The great detective stood perfectly still, and waited to see how a lack of action, on his part, might provoke Wood.

He did not have to wait long, as Wood began to taunt, "Come on, Mr. Holmes. It's cold up here. I don't want to stay up here all night. Are you too *afraid* to catch me?"

"Very well, Wood. I shall come and get you."

"You can't! Don't be a fool, Holmes," pleaded Watson.

"I must," replied Holmes, as he looked back at Watson. He then smiled and started to climb up a ladder that was fastened to the side of the roof from the fire escape to the top of the building.

The frost lay quite thick on the apex of the roof, making progress exceptionally dangerous for Holmes. He knelt down and slowly started to make his way along the rooftop, towards Wood.

Holmes felt his heart beating heavily, as he carefully inched his way along. His hand fell upon a loose slate, which slid out of place causing him to tip and loose his balance. He grabbed the top of the roof with his other hand to stop himself from falling off. He pulled himself back into position and held his breath, as he remained motionless whilst regaining his courage. When he overcame the shock of almost falling, he slowly continued along the rooftop.

Chapter 9

"It's a beautiful sight, do you not agree, Mr. Holmes?" said Wood. Holmes stopped and looked over to the murderer, still clinging onto the chimney, whilst looking out at the view.

Holmes looked out in the same direction as Wood and had to admit that it was a beautiful view. The lights emanating from the city shone brightly against the backdrop of the night sky. Below, there was a thin band of mist coming from the river but, otherwise, the night was clear.

When Holmes was about six feet away from Wood, he looked over to him and asked, "Have you any intention of coming back off of this roof with me?"

"I spent a great deal of time thinking whilst I was incarcerated, Mr. Holmes. The best games take a great deal of time to conceive and plan, and this one is no exception. The game's a head, Mr. Holmes. Remember those words? Yes, it was I who said those to you. I have been leading you along a path that I devised long ago. I have anticipated every move that you would make in my game."

"I realised that you were taunting me, Wood. It was obvious that you were leaving clues, like bread crumbs, for me to follow. But now, here we are on this roof and your options are, decidedly, limited. What do you intend to do, Wood?"

The murderer seemed calm, as he smiled and continued, "Every game has a winner and a loser, Mr. Holmes. You

The Dark Reckoning

have played your part in the game well, but now it is over. It is time to find out who wins."

Wood stood tall on the roof and shouted, "Play on, Sherlock Holmes," as he let go of the chimney, slid down the roof and fell off the edge. Holmes watched, in horror, as Wood fell through the air, his arms and legs flailing around and his voice screaming in terror. His fall was abruptly halted as he hit the top of a street lamp. The pointed top of the lamp pierced Wood's stomach and his screaming immediately stopped. Wood's impaled body violently twisted and contorted, as he tried to free himself. Blood spewed from his mouth onto the pavement and road below.

The onlookers on the pavement had all backed away, and all had their attention transfixed on the writhing body above. Blood ran down the glass of the gaslight rendering its glow red, as Wood continued to struggle.

As life started to slip away from Wood, his movements became weaker and slower. His head dropped and his legs hung still. The only movement was a slight clawing of his hands, but this, too, soon stopped. His arms and legs started to twitch for a few seconds and then he became perfectly still.

Holmes, witnessing this spectacle from above, knew that Stephen Wood was dead.

Chapter 10

Chapter 10

Curling veins of smoke rose from the pipe clasped in Sherlock Holmes' hand, as he sat in his favourite armchair at 221b Baker Street. He looked over at Dr. Watson, who was standing by the window and looking out at a bright, sunny morning.

"Watson, I have been thinking about this case, or 'game', as Wood described it. Just before he fell to his death, he mentioned that every game has a winner and a loser. He went on to say that it was time to discover the winner of his game. It seems to me that, ultimately, he was the winner."

The Dark Reckoning

Holmes puffed on his pipe, waiting for Watson's response.

Watson turned from the window and asked, "How can you say such a thing, Holmes? After all, Wood is dead."

"That is true, Watson," smiled Holmes. "However, his game was about making a travesty of our legal system. He even wrote that the '*law is devoured*' in one of his notes, and he managed to manipulate events to make that statement true."

"I fail to understand. Would you please explain yourself?" asked Watson, with a puzzled expression on his face.

"As you are aware, Watson, there were six intended victims that Wood had planned to kill, including us. All six played their respective roles within the legal system, resulting in Stanley Wood being sentenced to death. The six people abided by the law and received no reward for doing so. The law also judged Stephen Wood insane and he was placed in an asylum, accordingly."

"I still don't follow you, Holmes."

"This is where the travesty occurs, old man. The same legal system, that was indebted to the six people, decided Stephen Wood was sane and, subsequently, released him. In doing so, it, effectively, sentenced the six people to death. So, it proves that we have a foolish legal system that, unwittingly, assisted Stephen Wood in his dark plan. Six people helped the legal system to sentence a maniac to

Chapter 10

death, and the same system allowed four of them to be murdered."

"Come now, Holmes. You can't believe that. After all, we are still alive. That proves that Stephen Wood didn't achieve his objective."

"Are you certain, Watson? Perhaps we were meant to escape with our lives. When Wood told me that his game was over, he realised that I knew he had won. I believe that he always intended to kill himself; it was the final part of his game. I believe he was well aware that our final encounter would be his day of reckoning. He had planned to either kill me, or take his own life."

"Why would he do such a thing?"

"After failing to kill me, his other option was to ensure that I should live with the knowledge that I could never catch him. He knew that his game was over, but that mine would not end if he, ultimately, evaded me. I believe that is why his final words were 'play on, Mr. Holmes'. He knew that I would play on. He left this world with the satisfaction of having escaped justice. At the same time, he knew that I will never be deterred in my endeavours to catch criminals. Perhaps, his final words were a compliment to my enduring tenacity for fighting crime."

Watson wondered how his friend's mind always managed to make such amazing connections when interpreting evidence. He had learned a great deal having helped Holmes work on many cases, but he could never see things in the same way as the great detective.

The Dark Reckoning

A small smile broke out on Watson's face as he remarked, "Holmes, have you considered the fact that Stephen Wood can no longer harm anyone? He will never again be a burden to the state, or to society, in general. That is in no small part due to your efforts, so I believe that it is *you* that won, not him. Also, we are now in a position to inform Miss Spencer that her sister's killer is now dead."

Holmes glanced up at Watson and a smile broke out on his face. "You are quite right, old fellow. Wood has gone and the world is a better place for it. We will go and inform Miss Spencer of the news, shortly."

Holmes settled back in his chair, feeling contented, as he watched the curling veins of smoke rise from the pipe he clasped in his hand.

Printed in Great Britain
by Amazon.co.uk, Ltd.,
Marston Gate.